OWLHOOT NIGHTS

OWLHOOT NIGHTS

by
Vic J. Hanson

Dales Large Print Books
Long Preston, North Yorkshire,
England.

British Library Cataloguing in Publication Data.

Hanson, Vic J.
  Owlhoot nights.

  A catalogue record for this book is
  available from the British Library

  ISBN 1-85389-913-5 pbk

First published in Great Britain by Robert Hale Ltd., 1998

Copyright © 1998 by Vic J. Hanson

Cover illustration © Faba by arrangement with Norma Editorial S.A.

The right of Vic J. Hanson to be identified as the author of this work has been asserted by him in accordance with the Copyright, Designs and Patents Act, 1988

Published in Large Print 1999 by arrangement with Robert Hale Ltd.

Dales Large Print is an imprint of
Library Magna Books Ltd.
Printed and bound in Great Britain by
T.J. International Ltd., Cornwall, PL28 8RW.

One

They came by night as their kind would have been expected to do, but their arrival was unexpected as there hadn't been any bad trouble in Sandela territory for a long time, though this fact might have seemed unusual when taking into consideration the area was so close to the border and the badlands.

Still, the town of Sandela, which lay in the centre of the area which had been dubbed the Sandela Strip, had in recent times gotten itself a tough law enforcement agent and a bunch of equally tough deputies with a wide bailiwick.

Abel Codine was a sort of county sheriff and sometimes acted like a regular despot, but his clean-up rate was the envy of many a lawman in the wide south-west territory.

He had 'posted' a few hardcases out of town and they hadn't been seen in the area since. He had killed two drifters who had made a somewhat inept attempt to rob the local bank. This case couldn't have been called 'bad', of course, as it was on the side of the town and the two dead men had been strangers anyway. In the ranching community things had been peaceful and drovers visiting town were mighty careful where they put their Ps and their Qs.

So things rubbed along pretty smoothly till the owlhooters came in the night and, just to demonstrate that they meant business, hit one of the medium-size spreads and ran off a sizeable bunch of cattle.

Two night herders got in their way and they killed one of them with two bullets plumb in his chest. One would've been enough. The second man was kicked in the head by a horse and they let him lay. Maybe they thought he was dead too, or they just didn't care one way or the other.

Anyway, before passing out he got a look at one or other of them. He said they were masked, sort of half-hoods across the tops of their faces with eyeholes cut out.

Sheriff Codine said flour sacks maybe, and that wasn't particularly original. The bunch had acted like professionals, though. And, what's more, they'd had a good start. They'd either got a very slick hideyhole for themselves and the beef, or the prairie had just opened up and swallowed 'em whole.

The cowboy was buried on Sandela's Boot Hill. His erstwhile pard got over a mighty headache and went back to his chores. The ranching community put out more night riders. Nothing else happened, and things began to get back to normal. But then, a few months after the first raid, and when folks were beginning to forget it, the owlhooters struck again.

They changed their tactics and hit three of the smaller ranches in one night with savage and bewildering speed.

Despite their ferocity, however, they did not have things all their own way this time, and that was because a feller called Dack Simms happened to be wide awake in the middle of the night and pacing the floor with a raging toothache.

Dack had the smallest spread of the three, if indeed the place could be called a ranch at all, with Dack being a sort of horse-dealer an' all. One of the bigger ranchers whose land ran to the edge of Dack's patch had referred to him as 'that goddamn sodbuster'.

Carrying a sawn-off shotgun—not exactly the kind of armoury to be owned by a regular law-abiding cuss—Dack had rushed out of his leaning, frame abode screaming with pain and rage.

One of the rustlers had turned a white, garishly decorated face towards him, and Dack had filled that face with a charge, blown it apart mask as well, shredding it. Again, though, the others had gotten clean away with three horses and a small bunch of Dack Simms' cattle to boot. Well, all of 'em it seemed. But Dack bemoaned the lack of the three prime horses most of all.

Sheriff Codine took a look at the dead rustler, who was unrecognizable anyway and, apart from his weapons—and he had quite an array—possessed nothing with which he could be identified: a pack of Bull Durham and some rolling papers, a toothpick of tarnished metal, a little fat roll of greenbacks tied with string, three gold coins, a pearl-handled pocket knife (this beside a wicked-looking bowie tucked in back of his belt), a torn blue kerchief with red spots ...

Abe Codine said, 'A feller like him wouldn't carry papers. Things like that while on a job. Maybe he couldn't read anyway. He's bound to have a place where he could light down, leave things. I knew a road agent who used to leave most everything with his favourite whore when he went out on a job.'

'What happened to him?' asked Dack Simms.

Codine said, 'I killed him. It was a long time ago.'

The sheriff wasn't all that old, though markedly older than his deputies who were ranging around, half-bent, kicking things petulantly in the new-morning light. Their boss could have been called craggy-looking and had a black moustache which matched his thick black hair which, however, had wings of grey at the temples.

In age, Dack Simms was kind of midway between the sheriff and his deputies and was a lean, stringy-looking cuss who looked more doleful now than he usually did.

He brightened somewhat when Codine handed him the cash taken from the dead bandit.

'Might compensate for your loss.'

'Might at that.' Dack was far from being the effusive kind.

The lawmen rode off, looking for sign. Dack began to look doleful. His bad tooth was pestering him again.

At another spread there were two other dead men but they weren't rustlers; they were night herders who had both been shot in the back. Their pards hadn't been anywhere near them, hadn't even heard the shooting because of the pounding of the running cattle.

It was as if the owlhooters had figured to leave another token behind. Or maybe it had been revenge because of the man they had lost at the Simms' place which had been the first they had hit.

The three spreads had been in a sort of half-circle. The attacking bunch had seemingly come from the direction of the badlands and the Mexican border. Any of the three small ranches could have been the first.

The third ranch had lost cattle but no men. The bunch had hit the cattle from behind and the night herders—four of them in this case, more than were usually out there—had had to scramble to escape being run down by the startled beeves.

The noise of the cattle had been the only sound the cowboys had heard. It didn't seem that the rustlers had used their guns at all, just waving capes and blankets and ropes, making shrill noises, using the pressure of wildly galloping horse-flesh.

Only one man had spotted the raiders and he hadn't seen their faces, didn't know whether they were masked or not, though of course they were. He had been the first to fire a shot and he hadn't hit a thing. The distance between the three spreads was probably too far for shooting to be heard from one to the other. Nobody had heard the boom of Dack Simms' sawn-off.

The sheriff and his two deputies cut sign until they hit the badlands. Then they lost everything on the sparse ground, among the ancient-looking rock outcrops, the cacti, sand, occasional Spanish bayonet and chaparral.

They had to give up.

Dack Simms buried the body of the dead rustler in land not too far from his house on the edge of territory belonging to his rich neighbour, the owner of the biggest spread in the territory who had been trying to buy Dack's land, without success.

Dack even put a tidy-looking pile of rocks to mark the grave and go some way to prevent predators digging it up. He didn't go as far as to cut a cross.

His neighbour took umbrage and had the rocks removed. 'Pure damn' spite,' remarked Dack dolefully.

The neighbour didn't go to the length of having the corpse dug up and replanted in Dack's patch. He was heard to say, though, that if it was the last thing he did he would get rid of that goddamn sodbuster.

Sheriff Codine had a short rest then he gathered all of his deputies together, five of them all told. He only left one of them in the jailhouse together with the old semi-drunk who served as jailer from time to time. There was nobody in

15

the hoosegow now, not even one of the old jasper's drunken friends. But, with the sheriff and the rest of the boys out of town, well ...

The sheriff said he was going to get that border bunch—that was what folks were beginning to call them. Even if he had to go plumb out of his jurisdiction—wherever that was.

The first night after the law party had gone, leaving behind a seemingly peaceful Sandela, was when the border bunch hit the town.

Two

The funerals were first, the buryings of the two cowboys killed by the rustling owlhooters. Their graves were prepared side by side, only a few feet between them.

There couldn't be any delay as now the weather was exceptionally hot, with a humidity that made the sweat pop from a body's skin.

The boys' boss was there but not so many of their actual friends. They were out watching, trailing. The border bunch had never struck by daylight. But you never knew ...

Sod-buster Dack Simms had come in to have his bad tooth pulled and afterwards, even at the graveside, he looked a whole lot less doleful.

Townsfolk and waddies were at the graveside, but not the law. The sheriff and most of his deputies were out a-hunting human wolf kind and the youngest deputy and the old jailer were watching the jailhouse.

With a lot of the populace on Boot Hill the town below was quiet. It would've been a good time for the bandits to hit the place. But maybe, like many of their kind, they preferred the night, the masks, the anonymity.

Maybe they came from nearer home and that was why they covered their faces. The West was full of titles, many of them spurious. But the robbing and murdering gang remained 'The border bunch', not a very imaginative title but fitting.

At first the funerals went off fine. Just one shindig really, a sort of collective burying. As the graves were so close together, a single peroration was all that was needed and the tall preacher, who had a summer cold that made him sound like a broken foghorn, didn't waste any time. As things turned out, his brevity was fine.

The sun, though it wasn't yet at its zenith, was like a red gong resounding, beating on the heads of the gathered mourners. The males were glad to put their hats back on their boiling heads. There was only an atom of breeze so the females, and they were in the minority, didn't have to hold on to their bonnets.

The change in the weather came as the congregation was moving away from the graves, going downhill, leaving the diggers to finish their task. The rattling hearse, which had seen better days, was pulled by four horses. There was only one black, and he had a white blaze under his chin. He was a stout stallion with an aggressive nature and if any of the four beasts could've been called the leader he was the one.

The clouds came swiftly and rolled across the sun, blocking it out. But, strangely, the heat intensified, was like the breath of a thousand furnaces.

Thunder rolled and forked lightning split the clouds. One of the two lead horses screamed and pranced. His partner, who happened to be the black stallion, turned furiously and bit him in the shoulder.

The injured beast, another stallion a mite smaller than the black and of a spotty dun colour, screamed again, this time with pain, and bolted.

The rain came down like a wall and the swaying hearse was hidden from the downhill-scrambling mourners by a grey veil. They found the driver at the foot of the hill. The ground was already turning to mud as the rain drove and splashed into it.

The hearse was come upon lying on its side in the middle of Main Street. It looked like a pile of shattered timber. Three of the horses were still running. The black horse was drinking at a trough while the rain beat down on him, streamed down his sleek flanks.

The driver, limping after his fall, went over to the beast who turned, teeth bared, eyes rolling wickedly, and tried to bite him.

'To hell with you then,' said the driver and let him be.

Everybody sought shelter. The ground was like a huge quagmire, the main street and its tributaries, the slopes of Boot Hill streaming like bursting creeks. But because of the grey veil of the rain the townsfolk weren't able to see those slopes now or the two gravediggers, their task only partially done, running, tumbling, scrambling down them.

The rain continued with steady violence. Thunder clapped and rolled and lightning spasmodically lit the deathly near-darkness.

The saloons and cantinas did a boom trade for the rest of the day and into the evening while the rain set in as if it would go on forever.

Many folk went to bed with a skinful of booze that night and the rain didn't keep them awake. It didn't by then fall with so much violence but steadily, with a drumming monotony.

Actually, the border bunch didn't have to hit the sleeping town of Sandela, they just had to drift in, swathed in slickers against the rain and masked like ghosts, not a soul in sight under the dark skies, only them, like mocking, unworldly creatures of the elements.

The young deputy was Bill Legwell. Not a common surname, but one easy to remember. His old pard, who shared the law office with him now, was a different can of molasses altogether. He was of Polish extraction and, as far as most of the townies were concerned (they were an illiterate bunch), his name was unpronounceable.

Like many Westerners he had his peculiarities, one of them being that, drunk or sober, he never went out without toting an old Henry rifle, using it most times as a sort of walking stick, as he toted a gammy leg also, a souvenir of his horse-breaking days. He had never been known to shoot the rifle. Folk remarked that he surely couldn't have it loaded or he'd be like to blow his foot off one day.

But the long gun gave him a name: everybody called him Ol' Henry.

Ol' Henry was good with horses, but he didn't ride them much like he used to. He did odd jobs and one of these was as part-time jailer.

Deputy Bill Legwell liked the old man, who had come to the States as a child and talked good American, better than most sometimes, could read and write well, maybe had had a good education. Although most of the townsfolk wouldn't have gone along with that, and some of them looked upon the veteran as a figure of fun, Bill thought Ol' Henry was a sort of mystery.

Bill himself was born and brought up

in Sandela and was the only child of a widow-woman who lived in a neat frame house on the edge of town. It was an old town as Western townships go and bigger now than it had ever been. Bill's father had worked for the big spread outside town and, instead of sharing the bunkhouse with other rannies, came home to his young wife most nights.

He had been killed in a cattle stampede on one dark, very stormy night. His son, William, had only been four years old at the time, but he always remembered the limp, lifeless figure of his dad being brought home in the rain. Since then a stormy night often brought that memory back to him.

His mother had never married again. About a year after her husband's death she'd taken up with a travelling drummer who visited the town from time to time. The man had wanted her to go away with him to his home in Kansas City, and the boy too. She hadn't been able to do that and finally the man, whom her son Bill remembered as a jolly character, had gotten himself new territory and the two people had said an amicable goodbye, hadn't seen each other since.

Just after this, Abe Codine became sheriff of Sandela, the previous lawman expiring after a virulent fever.

Codine began to pay court to the handsome widow-woman, Beth Legwell, and that was the way it was now. Before he became a deputy, Beth's son, young Bill, had worked in the local armoury and learned a lot about guns and how to use them, although he was certainly not of a pugnacious nature and hadn't even been in a fight since he left school where he'd behaved like most normally intelligent boys would: he had spirit but no malice.

So, yeh, he knew guns. Still an' all, there were lots of folk who, naturally it seemed, figured that Sheriff Codine had made deputy of Bill because of his relationship with the boy's mother although, if truth was told, she hadn't been keen on the deal.

Of course, Bill had thought it great. He was peeved now, though, that the sheriff seemed to be using him as a sort of convenience, no more important than Ol' Henry, seldom taking him out with the rest of the boys. Bill always felt edgy on stormy nights and now he didn't take much interest in his old friend's chatter, interesting though it might be.

He rose from his chair and said, 'I guess I oughta go make the rounds.'

Ol' Henry said, 'What, in this? Don't be stupid, boy.'

'Don't call me "boy",' said Bill automatically, ignoring the 'stupid' bit.

He strapped on his gunbelt, donned his slicker and the wide-brimmed Stetson he invariably wore. He opened the door. The storm was playing itself out a bit, but the thrumming of the rain was a drumming, steady monotony.

'Not fit for a damn' turkey,' grumbled Ol' Henry.

It was doubtful that Bill heard him. The door closed. 'Young jackass,' snorted the old man and lit his pipe. Law-doggin' on a night like this wasn't bad. He liked talking to young Bill; but being alone was good, too, and he had plenty memories.

Main Street was a river of mud and Bill Legwell kept to the boardwalk on the jailhouse side of the street, which was the best side. He had to step carefully on his high-heeled riding boots, for the sidewalk was slippy with water as well as being splintered and uppity in places well trodden by heavy boots such as his own.

There was no wind and he was glad of that. If that was blustering at him as well he would indeed go back to the light and cosiness of the office and to hell with the night rounds.

Lights showed only here and there on the street and they were dim in the rain.

Nobody seemed to be moving around.

There was a dim light in the depths of the biggest rathskellar but no signs of movement there. And no sound except of his own bootheels and the steady thrumming of the rain.

That old coot Henry had been right *all right;* but for Bill to reappear back in the jail office so soon would give the old bastard a chance to cackle and crow and Bill wasn't in the mood for that kind of levity right now.

He ploughed on. He remembered Abe Codine telling him that on the night rounds it was best to walk in the edge of the street rather than on the sidewalks. That wouldn't stop a bushwhacker taking a pot at you from a window, door or alley, but it would certainly stop anybody coming at you with a knife or another silent weapon. Hell, walking on the street gave a man more room anyway, Abe had said.

I'd need a damn' canoe, thought Bill now, or a high seat on a plough, or a damn' sled on stilts. He was still grinning when he thought he saw, through the grey veil of the rain, horsemen moving at the end of the street.

Cowboys going home, he thought. He hastened his steps, hoping to bid them goodnight. Jehu, it was a hell of a night for riding and that was a fact.

He went past the saloon. Nothing moved in the glow of light in the interior of the barroom. Past the batwings there was an alley where the law often trawled for drunks who might become aggressive.

Automatically, Bill glanced into the alley. He saw the man and the man came at him, something gleaming dully, swinging in his hand.

Bill lifted his slicker, scrabbled for his gun, didn't make it: the blow hit him with stunning force on the side of the head. A dark blanket descended, covering him ...

Three

The bunch had taken all Dack Simms' horses and cows but had missed the burro called Alberto who always slept in the shed that had been a privy until the top half of it had been taken off by a strong northerner.

Alberto actually belonged to Dack's only hand, and a not particularly permanent one at that, an elderly Mexican named Esteban who had an alarming penchant for strong drink, a-roving and a-bragging, full of tales of the days when he was a famous *bandido*, the truth or untruth of which nobody had been able to figure.

When sober and on the job, Esteban was a hard worker and Dack, having a sneaking affection for the old cuss, put up with his irritating absences.

Esteban had been absent when the rustlers hit the spread. He was still absent, and been missing longer than usual and Dack had begun to wonder what had happened to him. Had he maybe, on his way back that night when the three small ranches had been hit, run into the perpetrators of those outrages?

Dack had been in town for the funerals of the two cowboys who had been brought to death by the night-riding, murderous bunch. He had been tracking since, but without success. Stolen stock and murderous men appeared to have vanished into thin air, once on hard ground leaving no traces at all.

Then there was the day of the big storms, a time when the weather wasn't fit for man nor beast—or mourners on Boot Hill. Dack had planned to go into town and look for Esteban, but he held off. In the evening, the downpour seemed to lessen somewhat and Dack threw a blanket over the knobbly back of Alberto the burro and said, 'C'mon, yuh cantankerous crittur, get movin'.'

Even Esteban couldn't always make Alberto behave. He eyed Dack balefully in a sidelong way and the man kept away from his yellow teeth and, from a fairly safe distance, prodded him with a long, stout, peeled stick which Esteban kept in the shed.

Reluctantly, Alberto went out the door, stepped in a puddle and got his feet wet, got his ears soaked by the rain and backed.

'Damn you,' ejaculated Dack and climbed swiftly on to his back—Alberto wasn't very high anyway—grabbed the soiled rawhide that was always loosely attached round the fractious beast's neck and, with the other hand, whacked him solidly on the rump with the stick.

Alberto, who could move fast when things took him that way, shot from the shed as if from the mouth of a cannon and started out on an ungainly gallop, his sharp feet churning the mud. Dack almost slid off his blanket backwards, managed to right himself. Alberto wheeled around and started to make it back for the shed, wiggling his long ears petulantly to shake off the wet.

'No, you don't,' yelled Dack and whacked him again.

Alberto jerked his head round, yellow teeth bared, and tried to bite. But Dack knew all the beast's tricks, backed, whacked the burro across the nose with the stick.

Alberto suddenly began to move as if his ass were on fire, went in the right direction also.

The rain still fell steadily but not so spitefully. Dack was well-shrouded in an old serape and with a wide-brimmed hat to match. Alberto did some snorting but kept going.

'I guess you ain't so bad after all, you pesky throwback,' Dack said.

Although Dack Simms didn't know it, he

had a near match in town that stormy night: the night rider who had slugged Deputy Bill Legwell in the alley beside the saloon was a Mexican in a serape and a big sombrero—and suddenly there was another man just behind him.

The Mex had used the barrel of his gun to pistol-whip young Bill into unconsciousness, and now he reversed the gun, cocked it, aimed it down at the still form.

The second man reached round and grabbed the Mex's wrist, said, 'No shootin', you damn' idiot.'

The big-hatted individual swiftly holstered his pistol and, as if by sleight of hand, whipped out a knife, bent, stabbed downwards. The sharp blade found its mark before the second man grabbed the knife-man and slammed him back against the wall.

'Are you loco? The boss said no killin' either.'

For a moment it seemed that the

Mexican would turn the knife upon his companion. But instead he sheathed it in the back of his belt someplace.

'I had to stop heem. He ees a lawman. Look!' the big-hatted man pointed.

A star gleamed on the still man's chest.

'So? Leave him. This will be reported to the boss an' he ain't gonna like it. C'mon, we've gotta get movin'.' The sour-talking Anglo led the way. The Mexican mouthed an obscenity in Spanish and followed him.

The rain drummed monotonously on the still body of Bill Legwell.

The bunch had gone through the town like ghosts, the sound of the rain cloaking the sounds of their passing. In a sense they couldn't have picked a better night. A funeral, a drowning of sorrows (a prime excuse for a boozing get-together) then a-rolling, a-sleeping, a-whoring (then a-sleeping), *whatever*. But nobody, it seemed, with much of their wits left to them on this horrendous night.

The bunch didn't have all of it their own way of course—not all of them anyway—*only almost.*

They hit the express office by levering a window open, not waking anybody, taking the cash and some small bags of gold which the express-man had neglected to hide (one of the dead cowboys had been his cousin). The bunch also took the small safe, must have had a wagon waiting outside town, would blow the door later.

The express-man said there wasn't much in the safe anyway but, finally, was proved to be halfway wrong about that.

Anyway, the bunch got away with more cash from the bank after waking the banker and his childless wife, threatening to cut the man's throat and do the same to the female after raping her in various ways—they described these—before dispatching her also.

She was a comely woman. They argued a bit among themselves, their eyes gleaming through the eyeholes of their hoods, a bit out of range of the yellow lamplight by the bed. They decided they'd do the woman first and let the man watch. But by this time the banker had agreed to go next door with them, open the bank, the safes and strong boxes, give them all they wanted.

Afterwards two of them took him back to his bed and, with his wife, who hadn't been touched after all, left them bound and gagged.

They hit drinking places and a few other establishments where money could be found. They left an old swamper unconscious on a sawdusted floor, a wideawake whore with a duster tied into her mouth while her paramour snored beside her. They took jewellery and cash from the bordello, but maybe they should have left it alone as it was from there that the first alarm was given.

But by then the bunch was far out of town.

Four

Ol' Henry had been dozing in his chair. He thought he had heard something. Maybe young Bill returning. But there were no footsteps now—if that was what he had heard—and the office door remained shut.

The old jailer looked at his heavy battered gunmetal timepiece which looped on a thick chain across his vest. He was surprised at the time, must've been out longer than he thought. And it was certainly time that Bill returned.

The rain still fell. Not stormy as before, but still with monotonous steadiness. Somewhere water splashed. Some kind of an overflow.

Most everywhere would be closed now. Young Bill was a conscientious law-keeper. If he looked into the saloon it would be only to cheek that everything was quiet, as it seemed to be now after the funerals and the drowning of the sorrows. The keepers and denizens of the various booze establishments would have their heads down now. But maybe some late bird had asked Bill in out of the rain for a cup of hot coffee.

The old man waited a while longer. But then he began to get uneasy.

He rose, picked up his Henry long gun, opened the door, went through it, locked it behind him. Bill had a key.

The street looked like a river of black mud with huge puddles here and there, gleaming in the starlight, could've been bottomless. A witching night. No moon and the stars high in the sky.

Ol' Henry skidded on his heels on the boardwalk and almost went on his ass, almost dropped his rifle too, but reversed it, put it barrel-down, used it as a walking stick as he often did. Mud had splashed on to worn planks and the going was slimy.

The rain still thrummed, but then the oldster heard what sounded like hoofbeats, drawing his attention to the other end of town. He had long sight, only wore his specs for reading: many of his contemporaries couldn't read at all: Henry considered himself lucky.

He could see what seemed like shadowy moving shapes out there. Like ghosts, phantoms that appeared and disappeared.

Gone now.

And no sound but the doleful drumming of the rain.

Had he been seeing things? Had he been hearing things?

Tricks of the elements!

But suddenly there were more sounds above the rain, and they were real. And figures. No ghost horsemen, but figures running in the night and gesticulating and shouting.

Bill Legwell felt the rain. And he felt the pain. At first he didn't know what it was all about. And then he groped for the source of the pain, and he found it. A gash in his chest on the right-hand side. A tear in his shirt and cloth that was soggy with blood.

The rain had brought him to; the rain had cooled him. He turned his face up to it, remembering. He was in the alley beside the saloon. There had been a man in the alley and he had bludgeoned Bill, pistol-whipped him maybe ...

His head had felt like an empty bucket. But now the pain hit it.

Raising his hand made pain tear at his side and he almost passed out. He lay back and let the rain fall on him. He was lying in mud. He wondered if the mud would help his wounded side. That would be the Indian way.

How deep was the wound, how bad? The man had used a knife on him while he lay there. Had the man meant to kill? Why? Who the hell?—*what?*

He found that, despite himself, as if in

a dream he was rising. His one hand at his wounded side. Using his other one, his elbow, everything he had to help him.

He leaned against the log wall. He didn't call out. How many men had there been? Were they still around?

He was surprised to find that his gun was still in its holster. They must have been in an almighty hurry. He staggered out of the alley, and he heard voices.

A figure halted in front of him, and there was a big gun. Bill thought he recognized the man—as well as he could with bleary, pain-filled eyes. But the gun was a clincher.

'Don't shoot, old-timer,' he cried. 'It's me—Bill.'

He fell in the mud at Ol' Henry's feet.

The old man was bemused. 'The gun's loaded at that,' he said. 'But the muzzle could be blocked with mud.' Then he caught himself up. 'Goddamighty, son, what happened to you?'

But Deputy Bill Legwell had passed out again.

Folks ran around like headless chickens complaining, yelling to themselves.

Dack Simms thought he heard the sound of hooves above the rain. And one sharper sound like somebody hitting an empty bucket with a stick. Though it could've been a gunshot. But who would be firing a gun on a night like this?

Even the sound of hooves had died now.

Had the weather been playing tricks with him?

He didn't mind the rain so much now. He couldn't get any wetter. The sky was getting a little lighter, he thought, and the rain didn't blanket the high stars. Did you often get stars on rainy nights, he wondered? He couldn't remember.

He couldn't see anything around him, ahead of him, except the rolling prairie. Couldn't see far anyway.

Not far to town now. And the burro, Alberto, was, remarkably, being as good as gold.

Dack thought, what am I doing out here—me an' the burro out on a night like this? Looking for a boozy old Mex. Hell, I need a drink myself now.

A cantina might be open late, the one Esteban used for instance. Maybe he'd meet the old goat there—if they hadn't passed each other like ships in the night.

There were lights in the town, twinkling. He hadn't expected to see so many lights.

When he got nearer he saw the people and the horses. Then beasts and people were as one and, in a bunch, they were coming out at him.

Alberto, who for miles had been as tractable as Heaven—so tractable that Dack had wondered whether the beast had been sickened by the rain—became startled, took umbrage at the animals and humans bearing down on him in force and turned and bolted.

Dack, who didn't ride the burro nearly as much as old Esteban, didn't think the little cuss could move so fast, cutting into the ground like the forked lightning that had been seen yesterday. He'd always thought of burros—even this one—as plodding beasts of burden.

But this one—this one was moving like a goddamn trick racehorse at a county fair.

He tried to signal to the horsemen who were now his pursuers. Turning, he was almost flung from Alberto's back.

He let the beast carry him. There was nothing else he could do.

But again the little burro took him by surprise.

The rain at last was abating. Vision was clearer in the night. Even the stars seemed lower and brighter. And on the flatlands in front of them there was suddenly a shape, a large bundle in the wet grass.

And Alberto came to a skidding halt, almost throwing Dack forward in a nose-dive.

Dack raised himself upright, turned and waved weakly at the bunch behind him who were slowing down. Then he turned ahead again, looked downwards.

He had seen bodies before. Hugging the ground as if at the last moment they had sought desperate escape from the grim spectre, had sought to bury themselves out of sight, though not in permanent grave, only in a hope for resurrection.

This one was as dead as anything could be.

Alberto was still. Dack got down from his back and, as he did so, the bunch behind him caught up and a voice said, 'Eet ees you, *Señor* Dack.'

And old Esteban dismounted and came forward. The others sat their horses, staring, wondering, while the old Mexican and his younger boss squatted down beside the body which, like Esteban, was Mexican, his sombrero lying on the ground beside him.

'He's been shot in the back of the head,'

Dack said. 'Do you know him, *amigo?*'

'No, I do not think I have seen 'im before.'

More men dismounted and joined the two. One, bending closer, said, 'I think I saw him. I think he was one of that bunch.'

Dack Simms turned his head, said, 'What bunch?'

Alberto stood stone-still except for gently flicking big ears watching these ridiculous humans. He had no fear now of the thing in the grass.

The rain was gentle now and the men, huddled around the corpse, talked in hushed voices. There seemed so much to ask and so much to tell, but so much unknown and puzzling and dreadful.

Esteban, the philosophical one, rose and went to the burro and scratched one of his ears. Alberto nuzzled the neck of the human who was his real master and who smelled of spicy things.

Esteban said, 'What are you doing out

so late at night and on such a night, little *amigo?'*

Alberto did not attempt to bite him or kick him as he sometimes did—though Esteban was usually too quick for him—but nuzzled him harder.

Behind the man and the beast the voices became louder.

Five

Many voices told Dack what had happened in town. He might have said 'It figures', as professional bandits like the bunch that had hit his place didn't usually confine themselves to just running cattle, but he didn't. He was mighty displeased to hear that Deputy Bill Legwell had been bushwhacked, hurt. Young Bill was by way of being a friend of his, far more in fact than any of the rest of the Sandela law, except for Ol' Henry and he couldn't be strictly called law.

He was glad to learn that the old jailer hadn't been hurt also. He asked whether the sheriff was back (hell, he'd be here if he was, wouldn't he?). Fact was, the posse couldn't have run into the border bunch, could they, or the bunch wouldn't have been able to hit the town?

Unless they had taken care of the posse first.

Six men, and led by a fire-eating gun-toter like Abel Codine—nah, it didn't seem possible!

Then again, some of the townies said the bunch that hit the town had been a big one.

Later, Dack thought that these gabby individuals had been more than stretching a point. The marauders had come and gone pretty silently and swiftly. That was what Dack heard from Legwell and Ol' Henry when he got to Sandela with the disgruntled townie posse, none of whom, except maybe Esteban, likely to be a match for practised gunhands.

No, the real gunhands had gone ahead, Abe Codine's lawbunch. And where in hell they were now maybe the Devil himself only knew.

Deputy Bill wasn't hurt as badly as had been feared. The assassin's knife had been deflected by a bulky wallet, stuffed mainly with bills and 'Wanted' dodgers and such, and hadn't gone in deeply. The doc said if it had it would've hit a lung. That hadn't happened, but Bill would still have to rest up in bed for a while and keep as still as possible.

He was allowed to look at the dead Mexican the folks had brought in. He said, yeh, that was probably the cuss who'd slugged him—so had probably knifed him as well.

Why had the son-bitch ended up dead on the prairie, shot in the back of the head at close range, the heavy slug going right through and taking part of his face away with it?

The doc, a confirmed realist said dead was dead and a live one with a nasty wound had to be kept that way, made better. He called his young patient a few choice names and packed him off to bed again.

The dead Mexican had been stripped

of everything, including his gunbelt, and his knife obviously. His pockets were completely empty. He only wore the clothes he had once stood up in, rode in, killed in.

Otherwise, he was a wet, gory mess.

Dack said, 'Looks like a cold-blooded execution to me.'

A few townies looked at him curiously. This feller Simms, whom they didn't know much about, seemed to be taking himself a mite too seriously. 'This sodbuster' that the big rancher had called him.

'The big rancher' owned a spread easily the largest in the Sandela Strip, which was called the Sunburst. He was named Silas Deagle and was a thin, elderly cuss who looked like a preacher but was called by a nester 'a damned, shit-eatin' hypocrite'. The nester was no longer around, his homestead a charred ruin, Deagle's cattle browsing now on his strip of land which had a nice little waterhole on it.

Deagle had plenty of informants and had heard about the attack on the smaller spreads, had smiled thinly at the news. He let it be known that his boys should keep a sharper look-out. Nobody, though, had seen anything on the nights when the border bunch rampaged—and, it was said, nobody had seen anything since.

He had plenty of hands, some of them specially picked for other things as well as running cattle. If that bunch tried their shenanigans with the Sunburst Ranch they'd get a hot reception, he said.

Anyway, right now he had more pleasant things on his mind. His daughter was due back from college in the East. Her elder brother—Deagle had two offspring—had to meet her with some of the boys.

The young man didn't always see eye to eye with his father and blazed at him, scorned his taciturn and cold single-mindedness. Sometimes he hated his father, did all kinds of things to try and shake that seeming imperturbability. He and three of the boys met his sister at the railhead. She had always been a pretty child, but now her brother marvelled at her beauty. The rest of the boys, with the brother's watchful eye on them, treated her like delicate china, taking their hats off and calling her 'Miss Irma' as they helped her with her baggage.

Her handsome brother, Glyn, who had the town girls falling at his feet, was a noted *pistolero,* and short-tempered with it. Didn't do to mess with him!

Glyn had brought the surrey. Now he drove it with Irma at his side. The boys rode as a sort of guard of honour, keeping pace with the whirring wheels, the trotting pair of prime horses, the ranch's best.

They were halfway home when they saw the cattle and Glyn, who had eyes like a hunting falcon, said, 'Who are those boys driving that cattle? I haven't seen a bunch o' beef over there before, didn't know we'd got any this side.'

'Maybe they're strays,' said one of the riders. 'Being round-up y'know, Glyn. I can't tell who them boys are at this distance.'

Neither could anybody else, not even Glyn.

'You want me to go see?' said one of the boys.

Another one said, 'Maybe Mr Deagle tol' them boys to move that cattle an' drive 'em over to that section.'

Glyn said, 'They seemed to be goin' faster, like they saw us.' He hadn't answered the first boy's question, but now he did. 'You all go after those boys and find out what's what. I'll take Irma home.'

They weren't wet nurses, even for the boss's daughter. Or the boss's unpredictable son. They asked no more questions. One of them said 'Right!' and that was all.

They galloped after the distant bunch of riders and cattle and, as they did so, the whole bunch drifted over the brow of a low hill and disappeared.

The Mexican corpse was laid out on a trestle in the undertaking parlour. Ghoulish individuals came to take a look, though the dead feller was in such a mess he was virtually unrecognizable.

However, it had been noted that he had a nasty, crooked scar on the left side of his chest and that had remained fairly noticeable. Looked like a knife wound.

An elderly ex-drummer who had given up peddling and retired in Sandela had worked a lot on the borderlands selling dooh-dads to Mexican ladies. He now lived on the edge of town with an ex-whore of about his own age, like Darby and Joan. He said he'd seen a *pistolero* with a chest wound like that on the dead Mex and the feller had run with a bunch led by a *bandido* called Tico who had subsequently been shot to death by *federales*.

A man like that one would join another bunch, wouldn't he?

Still, the consensus was that the bunch

that had hit Sandela on that fateful night had been mainly Anglo. Maybe the 'executed' one had been the only Mexican.

'A bunch of sneakin' renegade *comancheros,*' one irate townie said.

His partner, still laid up in bed, had been pistol-whipped by one of the bunch and that had been an Anglo all right, unrecognizable, though, because of the improvised face masks all of the bunch had been sporting.

Deputy Bill Legwell was also still in bed, on the doc's orders. Bill hadn't said much, couldn't tell much. He was being visited by his friend, Dack Simms: he had been used to visiting Dack's place when out riding, then taking a coffee (Dack's special was like gunpowder mash and molasses) and having a chinwag.

Six

The Sunburst boys were on the edge of the badlands and hadn't seen hide nor hair of their quarry again. That bunch with the cattle had had a good start and had made the most of it, doubtless having spotted that they were being tailed.

Now the trackers were surprised to see riders coming towards them in the dusty distance, not a sign of beef anywhere.

The Sunburst leader, tacitly chosen, was the eldest and he said, 'Maybe they've stashed the cattle and are comin' back figuring to take care of us, shut our mouths for good.'

'Looks like we're outnumbered,' said another ranny. 'Looks like a half-dozen there.'

The leader looked around him, pointed

to an outcrop of rocks. 'We can't hide our horses, but we can hunker down there, fight 'em off from cover.'

He whirled his mount and the rest followed him, taking the horses further back before crouching down with their rifles, behind the rocks.

'Wait 'til you see the whites of their eyes as the man said,' remarked the leader and chortled nervously.

'We can take 'em,' said the second ranny.

'Sure we can,' said the third one.

They weren't just horny-handed cowpokes. They handled their weapons with a good measure of expertise.

They were young. The elder was not yet thirty, his companions considerably younger. One of these raised a rifle to his shoulder, levelled it. The elder knocked it down, said, 'Jackass! That's the posse. That's Abe Codine ridin' in front.'

'He's right,' said the third man.

They all rose slowly from concealment,

knowing that by now their horses would have been spotted. And the posse came on warily. The three rannies sloped their rifles, and the elder one raised one hand in a peace sign.

The posse reined in, fronting them. The sheriff and his deputies were damp and bedraggled, almost as if they had come out of a rainstorm, although the rain had stopped some while ago. They were scruffy too, for the hard ground of the badlands was already becoming dusty, returning to its pitiless nature.

The skies weren't particularly light, so maybe there was more storming in the offing. The posse looked stormy enough: they obviously hadn't caught anything or anybody. Unless they had been chased off, of course, and that hardly seemed likely.

'What you boys doing?' Sheriff Codine asked.

They told him, all speaking at once. And he said, 'We ain't seen no men and cattle.'

'They must've made some kind of a detour then ...'

'I guess we better go back ...'

'We'll go with you to the Sunburst,' Codine said.

The visit was short. The posse took coffee but didn't wash up. Silas Deagle was taken up with the return of his beautiful daughter, Irma, saw the posse and the three rannies in his office.

The elder ranny said, 'It didn't look like a big bunch. The cattle, I mean. We didn't figure how many men there were.'

'The cattle,' Deagle snapped. 'I want a tally. Tell Glyn.' Glyn was his foreman as well as his son.

'We'll get out again later,' said Sheriff Codine. There was no love lost between him and the rich rancher. Codine didn't say how long a break there'd be before there was any more riding.

As they sighted the town Codine said, 'Them rustlers. Didn't sound like the border bunch to me.'

'Who was it then?'

'Search me.'

The town was being put to rights since the rain. Some kind of passage was being made along the main street. But now the law discovered that it had much more serious things to think about.

Murder; mayhem; robbery. All happening while Sheriff Codine and his deputies had well and truly had their backs turned.

The stay-at-home deputy Bill Legwell had a nasty wound, and his partner Ol' Henry was drunk and mighty vociferous. But not nearly so vociferous as the banker, a pompous man, and his wife, and other townies who'd got in the way of the night riders and suffered injury and loss.

Dack Simms and his friend Esteban had returned to the spread, together with the burro Alberto.

Dack had bought a horse in town. Esteban already had one, his usual neat

Indian pony that had been with him in Sandela when Dack's place was hit and his stock run off.

Esteban was one of the best trackers in the Sandela Strip and now he wanted to go a-tracking. How could he find anything after all that rain Dack wanted to know? Esteban said he might just find something. Dack knew that if anybody could it would be Esteban. But he said, 'Hell, you ain't feeling guilty, are you, 'cos you weren't here when those bastards called? It was your night off anyway, f'Pete's sake.'

Esteban wouldn't be goaded, said, 'I'll go look anyway. I'll take Alberto—he has a nose.'

Dack had to let them go. The ambling burro and the seraped elderly man perched on his back: nobody'd pay them no mind.

They were out of sight when Dack had another visitor, coming in from another direction.

A girl on an almost pure white horse. Dack had seen the horse before, knew it

63

belonged to the Sunburst Ranch. But at first he didn't recognize the girl. Not till she reined in and spoke his name.

'Great Jehosophat,' he exclaimed. 'Irma.'

Though it wasn't generally known, they had been friends for quite a while, ever since the girl's pony had been scared by a rattler and had bolted after throwing his rider. She hadn't been hurt, just shaken, had gone back to Dack's place with him and rested and taken coffee.

She had learned that this man with the still, dark, but friendly face, the man whom her father had referred to as a 'sodbuster' was erudite and well mannered. The pony had returned, as frisky and amenable like nothing had happened, and the girl had gone on her way. But she had called again while riding on more than one occasion and yarned with her new friend.

Missing her, he had learned that she had gone East to college. He had thought of her as a sharp, pretty, intelligent kid. There wasn't a great gap in their ages but to him who, though still young had seen many things, she was an innocent. And a rich man's daughter to boot.

How in hell did a mean son-bitch like Silas Deagle get to have a daughter like Irma?

She was beautiful now, her fresh brown-eyed face set off by a rich fall of raven hair that the perky riding hat she wore did little to hide. Her little pony was gone: she, the girl, matched the magnificent white stallion.

Suddenly, as she dismounted, he felt at a loss for words, but he blurted something out anyway. 'I didn't know you were back. What did they learn you at that college in the East?'

'Some folks called it a finishing-school I think.' She laughed. 'It *finished* me. I learned things. I guess I'm now supposed to be a well-educated young lady. But I didn't ever feel I belonged up there. I came back and I'm staying back. I'm a Westerner, Dack, just like you.'

'A Westerner,' he echoed softly. He didn't think she should be riding alone after all that had happened in this territory lately. But he didn't say so. She had always been a somewhat headstrong girl.

'I'm so glad you're back,' he went on. 'C'mon inside.'

He let her precede him. She knew the way well. Her walk was elegant and very feminine. Suddenly the sight of her stirred him as he thought he'd never been stirred before.

Seven

Esteban passed a small grove of cotton-woods and then he was on the edge of the badlands and could see an outcrop of rocks just ahead of him. But past that outcrop there was only an expanse of flat space reaching on to the horizon, and a haze of nothingness, a depressing sight.

Esteban knew those rocks, had seen them before. They were shaped like four Mexican sombreros, of various sizes, and a couple of twin Eastern derbies of the kind that Esteban had seen the new railroad men wearing.

Although Esteban didn't know this, these were the rocks behind which the three Sunburst rannies had crouched watching the law posse, meeting them.

Esteban hadn't found anything on his

tracking. Maybe Dack had been right. And Alberto was getting kind of crotchety now, flicking his large ears, throwing back wicked glances from rolling eyes.

Although Esteban had full canteens and some grub and wasn't scared of the wastelands he debated about turning back. Then Alberto made a little startled sound and turned his head, but this time he wasn't looking wickedly at his master, was staring right past him.

Esteban had that feeling then: as if eyes were boring into his back.

He turned his head. Two mounted men were coming out of the grove of cottonwoods and approaching him.

'Easy, *muy amigo*,' Esteban said and he turned Alberto around.

Both the riders were Anglo, young, hard-looking. They were a mite smarter than average cowhands, waddies, drifters. They wore slouch hats with the brims pulled low down over their eyes but Esteban knew he would have recognized them had he known them. He was sure that he didn't.

One of them had a rifle tilted upwards, the muzzle resting against his horse's neck.

'Hallo, my friends,' Esteban said.

Neither of them answered. But the one without a weapon in sight looked at the one with the rifle and said, 'I wonder what this little coot's lookin' for.'

'I haven't a notion,' said the one with the rifle.

They kept coming, spreading a little further apart. The one with the rifle pointed his weapon straight at Esteban.

The other one said, 'What you lookin' for, little coot?'

Esteban lied, matching the speakers laconicism with his own. 'Lookin' for strays. You ain't seen a coupla mavericks wandering around, have you?'

'Nope!'

But then the rifleman spoke again. 'I know him. He works for the jasper with the little spread. Him with the mouth an' the shotgun who came out yelling at us an' got to shootin' an' plugged Frisky Joe.'

'Pore Frisky,' said the other man.

They looked at Esteban. The rifle-muzzle was like a fifth eye, the deadliest one.

They knew he was there. Like hell! But even while they looked at him, they talked about him as if he wasn't there.

'He's seen us. We'll have to finish 'im.'

'He doesn't know us. Hell, I don't know the ol' coot.'

'He might see us again. He'd be able to put the finger on us.'

'All right. You've got the rifle. You finish 'im. I'll take his black, greasy scalp.'

They were playing with him. Then they would strike him down like two cats with a rodent. The rifle was the challenge, that and the cold, calculating young eyes above it. The eyes of a killer who loved killing.

The mocking voices!

Esteban had had enough.

His long-barrelled Remington pistol was in the holster at his waist, covered by his tattered hide vest. He reached inside, drew smoothly the way his friend Dack had taught him. *Swiftly.*

But the rifle bucked and he felt the blow somewhere in his side. Such a small bullet; such a huge blow. He knew he'd lost his balance and was falling; and the gun was falling.

He hit the ground and there was no pain, just a sort of fog.

They were dragging him ... *dragging him.*

The voices seemed to be coming out of the fog.

'He ain't dead. Let us string 'im up in the trees, teach a lesson tuh them sodbusters an' cow-pushers an' townies ...'

'Hell, that burro! Catch 'im!'

Away. Then back. Footsteps thudding the earth, resounding in his brain. And the pain now was gnawing at him.

They were dragging him again.

'I dunno whether the boss ...'

'The boss ain't here, is he? Get this outa the way, then clear the other job.'

'It seems strange to me,' said Abe Codine, 'them rustlers taking only a small bunch of Sunburst cattle. And in broad daylight too. And then the other boys saying they didn't see anything.'

'But you didn't come back with anything either, did you, Sheriff?' said Ol' Henry, almost sober now but still showing the mean streak which only seemed to come out in him when he'd been on a toot.

'Those boys had a bigger start than us, you know that, you ol' goat. Hell, they saw the beef being taken away. They said it was only a small bunch.'

'But they didn't count the riders,' said one of the deputies.

They were all gathered in the law office, had fed, watered, changed, waiting for the sheriff to tell them what to do next.

'You think there was some kind of set-up?' said another deputy.

'Stranger things have happened. And I guess Silas Deagle is one of the greediest sons-bitches I've ever known.'

'Yeh,' they agreed. *'Yeh.'*

'Cain't prove nothin',' said Ol' Henry truculently. 'We'll go look for sign,' said Codine. 'You stay here, Henry. You keep him company, Hank. Bill can't do it.'

'Oh, hell ...'

'You do as you're told.'

'Guess I'll have to, huh?' Hank was yellow-haired, buck-toothed.

'That's right.' The sheriff flung the words over his shoulder as he led the boys towards the door.

'You be careful,' said Ol' Henry, sounding almost benign now. 'Deagle's got hisself a bunch o' sharpshooters.'

'Hell, we ain't gonna brace 'em. Just hunt around, pretend we're looking for that old miser's beef and the bunch who took 'em.' The door closed with finality.

'You got a bottle on you, Hank?' Ol' Henry asked.

It was twilight when Glyn Deagle and

some of his boys turned up at Dack Simms' place. He heard them coming and appeared with his sawn-off shotgun only to face an array of drawn weapons.

'Where's my sister?' Glyn demanded. 'We figured she'd come to see you. The old man wouldn't know or he'd have your hide, bucko.'

Dack slowly lowered the shotgun. 'She called in to say hello, but she left more'n hour ago.'

'Search the place,' said Glyn and his men dismounted.

'You shouldn't be doing this,' Dack said. 'I wouldn't harm Irma—you should know that.'

Glyn got down from his saddle and the two men faced each other. Dack grounded the butt of his sawn-off; Glyn holstered his six-gun.

Dack said, 'I would've thought Irma was back at the ranch by now.'

'She slipped out while the old man wasn't looking. She told me she'd be back before dark. I had to tell him that. He's hoppin' mad.'

The men came out of the house. There hadn't been much to search.

Dack said, 'I'll come with you.'

'We don't need your help,' Glyn was curt again. He led his men out.

Dack waited till all sight of them was gone. Night was falling. He saddled his horse, took his sawn-off and his belt-gun and rode out.

Glyn and his boys had seemed to be ranging. Dack went straight towards the badlands, didn't exactly know why he did so. Irma knew this territory well, but it had been a longish time since she'd ridden it. Maybe she'd got lost.

Maybe she'd had an accident. He didn't like to think of that.

He didn't sight the Sunburst bunch again. There was no moon but plenty of stars.

Ahead of him he saw the stand of cottonwoods on the edge of the badlands.

There was quiet all around and the stars gave a pale, eerie light to the trees as, his shotgun across the saddle in front of him, Dack approached them.

Eight

The two boys had all the luck. When they caught up with the burro the girl was stroking him, talking to him even, as if he were a lost child.

Her horse stood nearby, watching curiously, turning his head, and snorting when he spotted the other two horses and their riders.

The girl had called the burro Alberto as if they were old friends or something.

It was still light then; with a dark sun-glow.

'By all that's holy,' said one boy, no more than a profane phrase when coming from such lips as his. And: 'This is a lot easier than we thought it would be, ain't it?' said his partner.

'But is that the one? Is that the girl?'

'That's the one all right. Look at her, will yuh? There's only the one of her.'

'She's a beauty all right.' Tongue running over lips.

The girl looked up enquiringly, unafraid. They didn't think she'd heard what they said.

'This is Esteban's burro,' she commented. 'I wonder what's happened to Esteban.'

'We ain't seen anybody.'

They dismounted, approached her on two sides. Something in their attitudes seemed to warn her. At first she'd taken them for two of her father's boys whom she hadn't seen before. But they didn't look at her as if they knew she was the boss's daughter.

Did they know she was Silas Deagle's daughter?

'What do you want?' she asked.

'We want you, honey.'

Esteban had been hanged, that was evident.

Then he had been scalped.

The rope was nowhere near. There was no sign of the burro Alberto or any accoutrements. But who would treat a man this way for such paltry gain? Dack ranged, looking for sign.

He found nothing.

He closed the lids over the tortured, staring eyes. He could not do anything with the face. He wrapped the mutilated head in bandanna though, which concealed part of it.

He loaded his old friend's body over the front of the saddle on the horse he'd gotten from Sandela. Had that been so soon ago?

A good horse who didn't balk.

Esteban's hat was nowhere to be seen. Had his murderers taken it as a souvenir in which to place a scalp of black locks? Esteban had had a fine head of hair for a man his age, only tiny flecks of grey within it.

Who were those bastards?

Dack made his way back home, not seeing again the Sunburst bunch.

He laid the body down on the cot in the lean-to where Esteban, a roaming man, had spent so little time, only going in there to sleep.

He heard hoofbeats and went outside, shotgun at ready. In recent times that old gun had been like an extra arm to him: he didn't always carry his pistol, an old one too.

It was Sheriff Codine and his deputies on the owlhoot-hunting trail again. Dack had more bad news for them. And now he began to wonder whether Irma Deagle had been found.

He stood beside the sheriff as that moustached man stood over the small corpse. And Codine said, 'I guess whoever did this was strays maybe from that border bunch and Esteban came upon them by accident.'

'His burro wasn't around, and didn't wander back here either.'

'Strange. Looks like Injun work.'

'It isn't only Injuns take scalps, border scum do it as well. We were told that there didn't seem to be any Injuns with that bunch that hit town.'

'Howmsoever,' said the sheriff, 'we can't do anything for Esteban now, *amigo*. But the girl ... Well, we'll go to the ranch. Maybe she's turned up. I'd like to know.'

'Yeh, me too.'

'That's the first thing then. You coming with us, Dack?'

The reply was kind of surprising: a flat 'No.'

As the posse rode off Dack went into the house.

He crossed to the corner where an old oak brassbound chest stood, stout as the ship in which it had once belonged. He took a large key from his vest pocket and inserted it into the padlock, turned it.

The padlock was huge, bulbous, faintly rusted. The key stuck. It squealed as he used all his strength to turn it the rest of the way. He took the padlock out and it hit the floor with a dull thump as he let it go.

The lid of the chest squeaked as he lifted it, something he hadn't done for a long time. There was a smell of must and oil, the latter tangy, familiar. The canvas sack was on top of clothing and oddments.

It was the sack he wanted. He untied the leather drawstring and drew out the black oilcloth package and, as he unwrapped this, the smell of oil became more pungent to his nostrils.

The guns were first. The matched pair of pearl-handled Colt .45 Peacemakers. They hadn't brought *him* much peace, he reflected grimly. But guns were just guns. Even a beautiful matched pair like these. They were tools, just as good or bad as the man who used them. He had had things thrust upon him, things that he could not have avoided. But he didn't think that, after all he had used these large but elegant—and deadly—tools unwisely.

Too often, though, was that right? Was that why he had finally hung them up? No, more than that, hidden them away, locked them up.

He weighed them in his hands, a satisfying feel, something of the like that he hadn't experienced for years. No exhilaration now, though. And behind it all a shadow of sadness.

But he couldn't stop now.

He took out the box of cartridges and loaded the two Colts, which looked as pristine as the day he'd bought them from the old gunsmith in Dodge who added those little refinements, those adornments that were practical as well as elegant. No pair alike, he said, and that was a fact.

The gunbelt came next, and it had been made by the same hands, the hands of a master craftsman; and an artist too. Soft brown leather chased with silver; tight thongs into which cartridges could now be loaded, tiny pockets of death, holsters on thick straps hanging low, but not too low (the old man had measured his customers for guns as if he were doing a prime suit of clothes); a long, soft holster with a strap at the mouth, if such was preferred, and a button, and, at the bottom, a whang-string for the tying down—refinements that Dack hadn't always used.

He strapped the belt around his waist and stuck the twin guns in their holsters. The feel of it; the feel of *them*.

He took the heaviness away from him almost absently, not trying a draw, hanging the lot over the back of a nearby wooden chair.

He took the clothing from the chest. The outfit that in the old days had been part and parcel of the rest. Black shirt with red polka dots (he'd had a collection of these but now there were only two left and they smelled musty), tight black pants with Mexican pesos sewn at intervals down the seams, a dark red kerchief, a black and white striped cummerbund (hadn't seen one o' those for years!); and the boots, higher than the average riding boots, soft, tooled leather, high heels, spurs to match, but no spiked rowels: he had drawn the line at them.

All in all, though, an outfit to beat all, to remember, topped by a dove-grey Stetson with a snakeskin band. By cracky, he'd been a right prime show-off in those days!

But he was no show-off now—there was something almost symbolic about what he was doing.

He put the show-off outfit back in the chest, delved deeper, ruffling it, felt the cold steel of the rifle and brought it out. A Winchester Repeater, still considered a recent long gun and the best of its kind. He delved some more, found a box of shells in the very bottom of the chest. He loaded the rifle.

He closed the chest, figuring there was nothing else he needed from there. He fixed the padlock, locked it, stashed the key.

He still toted his old hand-gun, a Colt Lightning. The sawn-off shotgun was leaning against a wall. He had better togs than the workclothes he now wore. He decided to change. He hadn't used the old Lightning much, sometimes hadn't even toted it when he was out ranging or visiting the town. But he'd usually toted the shotgun. Yeh, a sodbuster with an old sawn-off.

Well, he guessed folks would think a mite differently about him now. Hadn't he killed a rustling night-rider with that old sawn-off the other night!

But this gear, this new set-up, this changed Dack Simms—that would be another new thing entirely.

He sat down on the wooden chair with the Winchester across his knees and his mind carried him back to the old days.

Nine

The man called Rupert Dacson could have been called a sodbuster, except that being kind of sickly he was averse to breaking ground for any purpose whatsoever. He wasn't stupid, though, so he raised pigs, chickens, ran a few horses, didn't mess with cattle much, had one milk-cow, always had one milk-cow.

He raised kids too, five of them, and if they became too much for him—he being sick and all—he went off on a booze, and his boozes were legendary. So then his wife, who was a strong woman, looked after the kids and the stock and always kept a good house.

Strange though it might have seemed to some folk, she still loved Rupert as much as she had when barely out of school they'd met each other for the first time.

They'd both come from what you might call 'respectable families' and had had a better education than had many of their contemporaries. Neither of them got the hang of writing very well but at least they could both read.

Her name was Drusilla and Rupert got her in the family way and her strait-laced folks threw her out. So the lovers married and moved West from their prissy Eastern near-city and raised more kids, and other livestock.

Two girls. Then the third baby was a boy and they called him Samuel. About then Rupert got sick with his lungs and was never the same again. But he still managed to father two more daughters.

As the son, Sam, got older Rupert left him more and more of the chores. The mother had her hands full with the four girls. Rupert went off boozing more often, sometimes staying away for days. He also began to gamble heavily. He moved around a lot. Different towns, different tables, wheels, set-ups of all kinds. He didn't always pay his debts.

Sam didn't know about the debts until one day two hard-looking strangers called at the house looking for Rupert, who owed them some gambling *dinero*. Despite Sam's hotheaded objections, Drusilla gave the callers all the money she could find. Their manner was threatening: they gave the boy hard glances, said they were still owed, said they'd be back.

At this time Sam had a gun he toted when ranging. Now and then he shot a jack-rabbit.

Often he missed. He began to practise more with the weapon, though at first it was a mite too heavy, a Dragoon Colt that bucked like a wild tiger tethered in a zoo.

The two debtors didn't return. Sam never saw them again.

He was coming on seventeen when the thing happened. He had been in scrapes.

He knew this lawless country, in particular the area round the nearest town in New Mexico, the town where Rupert had been a fairly regular toper and gambler but now gave a wide berth.

Rupert was at home, however, when the terrible thing happened—such depredations, such depravities were not common even in this near-lawless part of the wide West—a thing that would stay with Sam till the end of his life, a catalyst for all that he became and, ultimately, tried to put aside.

The four men came by moonlight, looking for Rupert. The day before he had brought back a few bottles of hooch with him, had used them, was sleeping-off the aftermath on a cot in the old lean-to in back of the house, everybody letting him be.

Sam was out back, saw his father stagger through the narrow, sagging door, fling a saddle-blanket over a horse's back and take off as if all the devils of Hades were at his heels. And well they might have been! The men who wanted him were roaring, murderously drunk, although at first the son, Sam, didn't know this.

He mounted his own horse, went after his father, a flying horseman in the moonlight, shouted for him to return. But Rupert's panicky, half-drunk frenzy seemed to have affected his mount: the beast galloped like a wild thing.

Sam had ridden his own horse a lot that day, had only recently got back home. The beast was tired, couldn't keep up the breakneck pace.

Sam couldn't hear hoofbeats ahead any more, couldn't see the fleeing apparition. He turned his horse about. He figured that he'd already gone further than he should've done.

He feared for the family back at the house.

He didn't even have his gun.

He saw the flames. His only thought then was: *I should have stayed!*

He should have let that cowardly drunk, his father, go, let him get away. He should have faced up to those men himself.

But, he told himself, he thought that they were just more debtors who would take what they could, roar drunken threats, promise to return.

Still, he couldn't convince himself. How could he?

The flames dazzled his eyes. Brighter than the moonlight. Brighter than hell!

He drove the tired horse. The flames grew. The smoke billowed back at him.

The two younger girls were staggering around in the yard, screaming, demented. He told them to back away, dismounted, ran to the pump with the dirty canvas bucket looped across it. He filled this and ran to the flames, cursing.

There were no men now. Only the flames fought him. He was driven back, eyes streaming, as the rear of the house fell upon itself. The men must have fired it before they left.

Earlier, he'd seen them briefly. Drunken waddies, he'd thought. But even drunken waddies didn't usually behave like this.

His gun was in the kitchen, would be useless now. He ploughed through what was left of the area. All ruined. The gun? That would be ruined too.

The front of the house was comparatively intact.

But it was a scene of horror.

Young Sam Dacson found his mother and his two older sisters. All three were only partially clothed, their nether limbs exposed, sprawled, grotesque. Filmy, bloodied shreds of cloth lay around them. They had been violated in many ways, frenziedly it seemed, before their throats were cut.

Sam was like a tragic wild man, hardly knowing what he was about. Eventually, he found himself out back again with the two younger girls, who sat on the ground holding each other.

Neighbours arrived, drawn by the light

of the fire. One of them had seen the four men, had recognized them. A clan called the Bellelays, father and three sons, who had once lived in this territory in a smallholding which had been just a base from which they launched their depredations.

They had finally, contemptuously, rustled neighbours' cattle close to home. Their place had been attacked. The Bellelay mother, an ex-whore, had received a stray bullet in the head, killing her instantly.

The father and the three boys had escaped, one of them wounded.

It was said they had vowed to return, wreak their revenge on the folks who'd driven them out, if catching them might have arranged a speedy lynch party.

The Bellelays had been seen further afield, off and on. Now one particular neighbour had a say. In a small outlaw town miles away he had seen the four Bellelays in a card game with, of all people, Rupert Dacson.

Nobody could figure where the Bellelays could have gone, after, under the pretence or otherwise of debt-collecting, they had finally got their revenge on this territory, though the Dacson family had had no part in the clan's banishment in the first place.

But it seemed that the Bellelays didn't think at all about right or wrong or any kind of simple justice. Folks called them animals. But they were worse than animals. Animals didn't torture, mutilate and rape their own kind.

The two girls were taken into the care of the local family, the goodwife of which had been a particular friend of Mrs Drusilla Dacson.

A posse was put together and young Sam Dacson insisted on going with them.

They found nothing and ultimately returned to their houses, their businesses, their offices, their jobs.

Young Sam Dacson did not return with them.

He kept looking, ranged the lawless places. He questioned, listened. He grew in many ways, not only physically. He was a dark, well-set-up young man with a set face and a quiet manner, with dark-blue eyes that were often strangely expressionless.

He looked for four men, one old, the others younger in rotation, the youngest limping from an old wound, the one he'd received in the fracas back at the smallholding where his mother had been killed, the rest of the family run off.

Derry Bellelay was only twenty, but still older than Sam Dacson. Derry was the first one Sam caught up with.

Derry's old wound had been pestering him and he had rested up with a cathouse girl-friend of his while the old man and the other two went off on a job.

Derry and the girl were sitting half-dressed when Sam walked in on them.

Derry was mighty cautious: his wicked old man had taught him always to be so. His gun lay on the edge of the bed next to the sagging armchair in which he sat.

The girl was seated in another, a wooden one next to him. This crib wasn't as devoid of furniture as some. The girl wasn't near the gun, which was next to Derry's right hand. His left was buried in the lower part of her flimsy pink shift which seemed to be the only thing she had on, except for furry slippers with pom-poms.

Both of the young people looked drowsy, satiated. But Derry was justifiably indignant at the interruption by a young feller he hadn't seen in his life before.

The visitor stated who he was, matter-of-factly, as if his presence there was all in a day's work. As it now was—for him.

Derry reached swiftly for his gun.

Sam had replaced his old Dragoon by another lighter-weighted Colt and had learned to use it well. He was smooth, quick. No crouch. No swoop. The elbow bent, the butt grasped, the weapon lifted, levelled, all in one smooth carry-on move.

A fraction to beat; but a fraction was enough.

The bullet bored into Derry's head in a spot between the eyes, just above them. At the close range its path tore the back of Derry's head out, and he went backwards, chair and all, the gun he'd managed to lift, but not enough, clattering to the floor beside the bed.

In the small room the gunfire had been thunderous. The echoes died and the girl was screaming, shattering the echoes again, awakening them. She had been spattered with her paramour's blood. She put her hands over her eyes and beat her feet on the floor and screeched, demented, expecting the next bullet to be for her.

She heard the bootheels, the door opening, then closing. She whimpered. She heard the key turning in the lock on the outside after the visitor changed it around.

The sounds went away. She tottered to the door and beat on it with her fists and started to scream again.

Nobody in town bothered much about a dead hardcase and a demented whore. When the rest of the Bellelay clan returned they were told what had happened, and young Derry was a mute and bloody witness. But nobody could tell the full story—and nobody seemed to be able to describe the killer. The cathouse girl was of little help. She kept mouthing 'monster', and that was it. They had their clients to consider, didn't want to give the place a bad name.

The killer had gone on his way. He waited elsewhere. He had a great patience. He had expunged some of the guilt he felt in himself. It was deep; it was still there; but it didn't harrow so much as it used to, though the big question remained unanswered.

Why had he ridden after his father on that terrible moonlight night? Was he a coward as his father had been?

Rupert had vanished as if into nothingness. Did Rupert feel guilt? Was he even still alive?

Whether or not, his son would expunge the guilt, real or imagined, for the both of them.

He didn't know whether the other Bellelays had a description of the man who had killed Derry.

The man, Sam Dacson, had given his name in the saloon in that town. Maybe somebody would pass it on.

Sam Dacson was driven, wanted to draw the rest of the clan to him, drive them to seek him, find him.

In Dodge he bought the twin pearl-handled Peacemakers, the outfit, the black trappings. He became a show-off pistoleer. He sold his other trusty Colt to a man in a bar, flourishing, making a show, making people remember him. Showing off the elegant twin Peacemakers too, he, Sam

Dacson, gunfighter in black.

He began to tell folks that he was looking for the Bellelays, that they should come out of their holes and face him. Would one of them have the guts? They usually worked as a team, *the clan*. Well, hell's bells, let them do that: he was ready for them.

Strangely, he came upon old Solly Bellelay much in the same way as he had Solly's youngest son, Derry.

During that time he met a friend from the old days who told him that his dad, Rupert, had fallen dead over a card-table in Prescott, after a violent coughing fit, spattering the pasteboards with blood. Natural causes, his old complaint. It was a wonder he'd lasted that long, considering the life he'd led.

Sam didn't grieve, *couldn't*.

Old Solly Bellelay liked his whores more than one at a time and, as he had an old friend who ran a bordello in Trenton, multiple meetings weren't hard to arrange.

Solly liked sex 'circuses', even taking part in them himself

The old man was just the start of it.

It was a set-up that Sam Dacson might have dreamed about, the set-up he had waited for, that he had set himself up for.

He had learned a lot. He knew about old Solly and his jovial, lecherous habits. He learned about Solly's friend, the madam. Quite by accident, a few words overheard in a bar-room, he learned when the old goat would be visiting his cathouse friend and her girls again.

And where Solly was his two boys wouldn't be far away; unless they were out looking for the gunfighter in black who had killed their brother and was goading them from remote places. But he was sick of waiting for them, burned with a desire to finish this thing for good and for all and find for himself peace of mind.

He found the place. He entered it and the

girls came forth, the brassy-haired madam at their head, inviting smiles like a myriad lamps in a garish setting. Such a handsome *caballero*, so wicked and dangerous-looking in his black attire.

Only the madam looked doubtful when he said he had an important message for Solly Bellelay. But before the brassy-haired frail could open her carmined lips another much younger girl spoke up, a petite girl with raven-black hair and roguish eyes. 'He's in the big room with three of the girls and I don't think he'd like to be disturbed.'

'I'm certain sure he won't mind, missy,' Sam said. 'It's very important I see him. Which way?'

The girl indicated the curving stairs. 'Red door first on the right.'

But then the madam spoke up. 'Maybe you ought to go see his two sons first off.'

Such luck, thought Sam, asked. 'Where would they be, ma'am?'

'Down at the saloon, The Coolie House, I guess. I'll tell Solly you called.'

'No need,' said the tall dark man and he was past them and up the stairs.

He was through the red door and four pairs of eyes stared at him, a tableau of surprise.

Such a tableau! Such a plenitude of female flesh. But the visitor had no interest in such right now. 'Quiet,' he said and he had a handsome gun in his right hand, another in the other side, like its twin but holstered to his belt. He was looking at the old man seated on a sort of *chaise-longue* with his pants around his ankles.

'Make yourself decent, old-timer. You're coming with me.'

'You!' It was an exclamation and a challenge. But the man was in no position to make challenges. He knew this young man in black would kill him if he had to.

'You girls stay put.' Sam locked the door on the outside and they were as quiet as mice as he shepherded the old man downstairs, only to meet questions there.

'Find the brothers and tell them I have their pa and, if they don't show themselves I'll shoot him in the head. I'll be down by the corral at the end of main street waiting for them.'

He turned to the madam. Fast. With both guns out, but one of them pointed sideways. At Solly's head.

'You holdin' this ol' goat's gun-gear, ma'am?'

Her eyes bugged under her brassy head. 'Yes, suh.'

'Go get 'em. And don't try anything funny or I'll shoot this ol' bastard an' you with him.'

The girls were about their business. The madam fetched Solly's gunbelt. Sam slung it over his shoulder. A redheaded filly appeared, looked startled, turned back.

'C'm 'ere, Trudy,' the madam snarled.

Cringing, Trudy did as she was told. She was given the message for the two

Bellelay boys and, looking fearfully over her shoulder, preceded the old man and the young black-garbed gunfighter through the door.

Ten

As was the case in most Western townships the cathouse was on the outskirts. This one had a halfway decent position at the end of main street. It was pretty convenient for Sam Dacson's purpose. There had been music. Now there was no music. There was a waiting. Soon the whole town would be waiting.

The corral was at the end of town not far from the cathouse and that suited Sam's purpose also. The quietness too, as he and the old man walked down the street, the younger feller having the muzzle of his gun near the other's spine. They were like two friends, maybe even a father and son, taking an evening constitutional.

The corral was a big one, almost a stockyard, and often stock was kept there awaiting selling or collection. At this time there was just a cluster of horses at the far end, the furthest from the street.

There were small barns and outhouses nearer to the street, and these were in darkness. Sam shepherded the old man to the nearest, which was not much bigger than a couple of privies knocked into one, and smelled that way too.

Opposite was another larger place, a small barn that smelled of livestock. But, like the smaller place, it was dark and empty, bars of moonlight only slashing across the open door, illuminating a section of hard dirt floor.

It was a moonlit night, and this seemed sort of appropriate. Sam remembered a horseman fleeing on a moonlit night such as this. But he pushed all this away from him. He made old Solly stand in front of him just inside the doorway with the sagging, broken-hinged door, and they looked out on to the main street washed with moonbeams and they waited; but didn't have to wait long.

There was nothing on the street, not even a cur dog or a prowling cat, when the men appeared, approaching. Not just two of them. *Three.*

And the third one had a silver star gleaming on his breast. *A lawman.* But he didn't call out or make any sign to indicate that the representative of the law was about to step in and avoid bloodshed.

'My nephew, young Jody,' said Solly, dully. 'We were visitin'.'

Three men walked abreast and then began to space themselves out.

'Turn around, old man,' Sam Dacson said and, when Solly did so, handed the old man his gunbelt, adding, 'Join your sons an' your nephew. Go on. Move!'

'You'll ...'

'No, I won't shoot you in the back. Move, I said.'

The old man shuffled out into the moonlight, buckling on his belt. The others halted, staring.

Sam Dacson had both his guns out. He waited till Solly was with the others and was turning, his gun in his hand. The others drew also—and that was when Sam opened up.

He fired twice, swivelling the gun slightly from left to right. Then he dropped on one knee, watching his bullets hit. One on each side of the old man, where the brothers stood, seeing the face of one blacken and shine in the moonlight. And he was falling.

The other one was staggering. I haven't got him good, Sam thought, fleetingly. But the man was trying to lift his gun level—while slugs zipped over Sam's head as the father and the man with the badge sent shots at him. The jamb of the door was split and dust and fragments pattered on his hat.

He rolled; and then he was across the space between the coffin-like structure, upended, leaning, and the larger shed-cum-stable.

He was partially in cover, though his hat had fallen from his head and was more in cover then than the rest of him. One of his legs was outstretched, vulnerable. He felt something sting it, as if he'd been bitten by a snake.

I'm hit, he thought. The pain came. He jerked the leg in with the rest of him. He was working on instinct now.

He could feel the warm blood running down the calf of his leg. He ignored the pain, dragging himself to a square of window, the moonlight streaming in, glittering on shards of broken glass on the inside of the window-frame.

Gun-slugs beat into wood but nothing came through. This was a much stouter place than the one across the other side of the small gap. Damn it, was he getting slow? He should have got across there without hurt.

But he was at the window. The men outside were aiming to the right of him, hadn't quite figured out his new position yet. He raised his head cautiously, had to crane it sideways before he could see them all. One man was down; still. The other one, his brother, was on his knees, struggling to rise, to lift his gun. Sam levelled, fired, saw the man jerk, then fall on his face.

The old man at the side of the second one was now in between his two dead sons and, ancient campaigner that he was, had dropped onto one knee, was firing. But his shots still beat into the wall to the right of the man in the shed.

The man with the badge, Jody, still upright, had bird-dogged Sam's new position, however. His shot smashed through what was left of the glass at the edge of the window and Sam started back, ducking his head, twisting, knives of pain shooting up his leg to his groin.

He spotted the gap in back of the building and he crawled swiftly, wormed his way through.

Coming round the corner of the building,

he took both men by surprise, although, almost by instinct, the old man swivelled his head, his gun.

Such was Solly Bellelay's position that Sam Dacson got him in the side of the head, spinning him around and putting his face down in the dust. He jerked. Lay still.

Sam flung himself forward and down and the shots fired at him by the badged nephew of Jody went over his head and, resting on one elbow, Sam sent a stream of lead back at the man from one Peacemaker, the other lying at his side. But he didn't need the second one. Jody went backwards, then over, legs kicking up frantically. Then his head hit the ground hard and he lay still.

Four bundles of shapeless clothing, Sam Dacson thought; and he felt sick.

He couldn't quite remember how he got out of that town—but he did.

As far as he knew no posse came after him or, if they did, they lost his trail.

He'd been trailed before. He was back on the owlhoot and worked by instinct, tying his wounded leg tightly, stanching the blood, keeping it up, way out of the stirrup that side. The blood congealed, broke out again, ran for a second time then settled down so that he was able to start going faster again as he had when he first left the town, though that had been hellishly unpleasant to say the least.

He rested up in some trees in the early morning, realizing with amazement that he had been moving all night, might have dozed in the saddle when the pain wasn't so bad. It was a dull ache now. He figured it was going to be all right, a flesh wound: he'd had 'em before.

He had biscuits and water, though he would soon need his canteens filling, must've gone at them drowsily in the night.

He found a settlement, took a room in a seedy little hotel, rested up. Then he went on his way again and nobody followed him. Who would? If folks had known he had killed the Bellelays—well, somebody had!—and the news was getting around as it would, who the hell could miss 'em?

The leg healed and he had no limp, just a crooked scar which itched from time to time.

He heard about the Bellelay killings. Then he heard that he'd been recognized and a price had been put on his head for the killing of the young law deputy called Jody.

Sam settled. *Sam Dacsun became Dack Simms.*

Then Dack Simms heard that there was no price on gunfighter Dacson's head now because the deputy hadn't been on law business but in sort of family feuding—and what a family! Maybe there hadn't been a price on Dacson's head after all, it had just been a rumour. Maybe some folks would like to give him a medal instead.

Speculations didn't bother Dacson either

way. He remained Dack Simms. He stayed where he was.

Different clothes. No fancy pair of guns. Different personality.

Eleven

Ol' Henry came out of the back door of the office. He was in no way drunk, not having had a strong wet since the morning.

Although his bad leg was a constant nuisance he knew he had to exercise it regularly in small doses. He figured that a short walk to the privy would suffice for this evening. Anyway, he needed to go.

He took the old Henry long gun, using it as a crutch, the barrel thudding in the soft ground. There was no rain. But the ground hadn't completely dried, particularly back here where there wasn't so much traffic, nothing but folks, and sometimes horses.

He had left the back door of the jail open. Anyway, there was nobody there now. He didn't know how long Sheriff Abel Codine and Deputy Bill Legwell would be.

Along the way, light filtered from the backs of other buildings.

There were voices but no words.

A drunken man was trying to sing. A woman laughed shrilly. A piano tinkled in the background as if played by ghost fingers.

There was a pale moon, the first for many nights, which shone across the littered ground, creating eerie shadows.

There was nothing moving, whether animal or human, before Ol' Henry went into the privy and came out again. But as he was crossing back to the jail office a door opened and a gush of yellow light spilled out, vying with the moonbeams, warming them.

By then Ol' Henry was in the long shadow thrown by the jailhouse but not in the narrow path of light from the door which he'd left slightly ajar.

Always inquisitive, the old man halted, remained perfectly still.

Two men came through the lighted doorway and he saw their faces. Young. One ordinary, almost boyish if hard. The other darker, vulpine, almost Indian-looking. The sight of this second one awakened a chord of memory in the watching oldster's mind.

The two men, obviously unaware that they were being watched, turned away and went in the opposite direction to where Ol' Henry stood.

He realized he had half-lifted his rifle. Now he grounded it. But still he waited.

He lost sight of the two men but soon heard the soft thud of hooves, which faded away in the distance.

The old jailer went into the office, closed the door behind him. Where in hell had he seen that one younker before, that face?

The answer to the question eluded him, nagged at him worse than his bad leg, he

119

thought, *godammit.*

The place from which the two young men had come, unspeaking, surreptitiously it seemed, was a dry goods store run by an immensely fat man called Twilight, because it was at this time of day that he, like a cat, came out to sit on his front stoop like a watchful, unspeaking buddha. But he did not, catlike, stay out after darkness had fallen, going back into his stores as soon as a plethora of lights shone along main street.

During the day he sometimes sat on a high stool behind his counter, beaming like an obese idol, but the seeming mirth not reaching his black-button eyes encased in pouches of fat.

Very often, though, he was invisible in the back of his establishment and his place taken by a vapid girl named Lucy who called him 'Uncle George'.

Some of the town's old-timers called him George. It was rumoured that he hadn't always been fat, that in his early days he'd run with a bunch of *comancheros* and ex-Civil War Southerners who were still fighting a war of their own.

Still and all, Twilight had always been a bit of a mystery, and legends were built on such.

Ol' Henry had never called Twilight 'George'—or anything else for that matter. He didn't much like the man, thought him a fat, unpleasant-mannered pig and left it at that.

A mystery? Why would two young men be visiting Twilight at night, by the rear door to boot?

Who were those two? Where had Ol' Henry seen the dark one before?

Aw, hell, maybe it had just been somebody who looked like him. The West was full of younkers like that, drifters, fly-by-nights, wandering waddies.

Silas Deagle's Sunburst spread seemed to be having new men all the time, more so now than ever. Were those two more of Silas's waddies—gunfighters even?

The dark one had seemed to have that stripe.

But where had Ol' Henry seen that face before, or one like it?

Twelve

Suddenly, Dack Simms didn't quite know what he was doing. It seemed that he was bewitched by moonlight—after the horrendous weather that had been almost the norm of late.

He sat in the grove of trees on the knoll. Not the grove of cottonwoods that lay adjacent to the badlands but another one entirely, one he hadn't visited for a long time, not even on his lonely night rides when he hadn't been able to sleep.

What had led him here on this night? He didn't know. He had seen nothing, found nothing. It was as if, in devious ways, he had been driven here, or *pulled* here.

He had had a companion on this knoll once on such a night as this, though probably earlier. Now it was late. He didn't know how late because he'd forgotten to bring his battered old half-hunter, which was his constant timepiece.

Still, he had changed his clothes, hadn't he? And he had the big guns strapped to his hips. Not fancy clobber. Not like in the old days: black like a raven; wicked like a marauding raven. He knew he would never again wear the black gear that had once been his sort of trademark.

But the guns were a different matter. And the clothes that went with them now. Certainly not work clothes. Hard-wearing, stripped-down, comfortable clothes that any gunfighter might wear. Certainly not the kind of gear that had been sported by a sodbuster called Dack Simms.

Now it was like those sodbuster days had never happened. His mind drew him back, *willy-nilly.*

The deputy hadn't been the last one. The young lawman Jody who'd been kin to the Bellelays and had backed them—oh, he could've been the last one, but he hadn't been.

Sam Dacson, exonerated from blame, had gone on a while longer. The black-clad gunfighter who had already been well known but had become doubly notorious when the news spread that he'd put down the hell-raising Bellelay clan, was the top now of the top guns of the West. And the top guns were jealous of their prestige ...

It had seemed a long time ago. But now it came back to the man who called himself Dack Simms as if it had happened only yesterday.

When he hit the ghost town he knew he was being followed. He'd thought at first that it was the law. But why would the law be after him now; notorious though he was, there wasn't a price on his head?

Only one man too. He was sure of that now.

The feller hadn't attempted to conceal himself in any way, had kept on at about the same pace as the horseman in front, hadn't attempted to catch up, hadn't waved or hailed—although maybe the distance had never lessened enough so that if he raised his voice he would be heard.

The man in front had thought of waiting for the cuss but then had decided, to hell with him. Some kind of a jackass.

The territory here was pretty flat, pretty bare. The ghost town was unknown. This wasn't a badlands, a no-man's land. But pretty close to it. Certainly not the sort of country for livestock or growing things. Maybe there'd been a mine or something near here and it had petered out.

The hard street was rutted, the buildings tumbledown, with sightless windows. A breeze blew the tumbleweeds; wild greenery sprouted through what had been wooden sidewalks. Off from the main and, it seemed, only street, tributaries were just dirt alleys where there was cacti and other twisted and prickly plants—the man could identify some of them—blocking the ways, climbing up the walls.

A sign creaked, lopsided, in danger of falling. The inscription upon it was illegible.

This was a half-building, looked as if it had once had a false front. Maybe the wind had long since carried it away. But this was the biggest building the first horseman could see, even without a false front. So probably it had been a saloon.

There was no hitching rack. Maybe that had blown away also. The horse, though, could be hitched at a splintered post while its rider entered the shell of a building, trestles across barrels, sagging empty shelves, after leaning batwings and glassless windows which let in light and bars of sunshine. A saloon, yeh, of a kind. But this town had never been a San Antone or Dodge City, or even a Tombstone.

There were a few tables and chairs. Everything was covered with thick dust.

This was a dusty, depressing area even outside.

The black-clad man with the twin guns sat down on a rickety wooden chair. He had brought a canteen in with him. He took out the stopper and had a gulp of brackish water.

He heard the hoofbeats coming closer. Then they stopped.

There was the soft thud of bootheels. They stopped too. The follower hadn't yet climbed on to the apology for a sidewalk.

'Mr Dacson,' a voice called. 'Are you in there, Mr Dacson?'

Sam Dacson rose, left his canteen on the small dusty table, walked to the batwings and pushed them open. One of them tilted at his push, scraped the floor, raising a small cloud of dust.

The follower stood just off the battered sidewalk midway between Dacson's horse and his own, a neat dun stallion with reins dangling.

But Dacson wasn't really looking at the

horses. He was looking at the man.

All in black.

Like a copy of Sam Dacson, notorious gunfighter and killer.

Twin guns too. Butts turned inwards ready for a cross-arm draw. Dacson could've thought, hell, this cuss is a bigger show-off than I am. Maybe he did.

About the same age as Dacson. Maybe younger. Similar build. Boyish face but cold. Eyes that seemed to stare more than they should. Fixed snakelike on the man who stood on the sidewalk just outside the batwings of the disused saloon.

'I'm Dacson.'

'I know. I should do. I've followed you long enough, heard a lot about you.' Thin lips; level, thin voice. Thin black moustache as if pencilled there. *Fancy.* But who wasn't? Two of a kind. Facing each other.

'What do you want?'

'I want you. I want you good.'

'Well, here I am. Why do you want

me? I've never seen you before. Who are you?'

'My name is Dale Consarn.'

'I don't know the name.'

'You will. But not for long.'

Impatience now. But a dawning awareness also. 'For Chrissakes, man, say what you have to say. I ask you one more time. What do you want, and why?'

'You think you're the greatest gunny who's ever lived, don't you, Mr Dacson?' The question was a jeer, and there was no wait for an answer. 'But you're not. I am. And I'm here to prove it. I'm here asking you to draw.'

'You're loco, boy.' Watching the eyes flare, their owner not liking the 'boy'. 'I'm comin' down into the street and I'm forkin' my horse an' riding slowly out of here, taking my time, y'know.'

'You're coming down on to the street all right, but then you're going to face me. And soon folks will be talking about me like they've been talking about you.'

There was no answer to that. Dacson went out into the street and turned to face the young man who called himself Dale Consarn. A name that might have caused merriment at times. Was that what ... ? No, that didn't seem likely. And no more time for cogitation.

'All right, my friend. Do what you think you have to.'

He was fast, was Consarn.

Dacson had always figured a straight-forward pull was better than a cross-arm, gave an edge. He gave Consarn a fraction, thought he had. But the man's gun-barrels were almost level, almost *killing* level when Dacson's own twin guns bucked in his fists and for one awful moment he thought he was too late.

But then Consarn was falling away from him and there was dust joining the gunsmoke. And then Dacson was looking at a dead man's heels.

A fool. A heartbreaking fool!

Using a jagged shard of timber, he

buried the fool just outside the town and put a leafy bough in the form of a cross over the grave.

Dale Consarn. Oh, yes, he would remember that name; he'd always remember that name.

Thirteen

From the past he dragged himself back to the present. The knoll. The trees. The moonlight. Remembering who had been with him the last time he was here. Irma Deagle.

It must have been earlier than this of course. Early on a new, moonlit night. They had met by accident out on the plains and had ridden up here and dismounted and sat and talked, just talked.

He heard the hoofbeats and he was back completely from the shadowy world where he'd been. He was here and now—and he rose and waited for the horsemen and they appeared.

Glyn Deagle and the boys from the Sunburst.

Ol' Henry was no great friend of fat Twilight and his niece Lucy but, despite himself, he began to worry about them.

It was quiet in town. The vestiges of late carousing and levity had long since faded away.

In the sheriff's armchair and his feet upon the desk, the old jailer found himself dozing off. But something niggled at the back of his mind, and he knew what it was.

Shadows. The shadows of two men silently coming out of a moonlit doorway and riding directly away into the silence of the plains.

And no sound now from the house, the stores where Lucy and her 'Uncle George' had their being.

Finally Ol' Henry rose, but this time he didn't take up his shotgun. He collected his trusty Colt and tucked it in his belt.

He closed the back door carefully behind him. Out here there was the silence of a very flat boothill with familiar shapes,

134

some of them ominous. The moonlight was benign.

Ol' Henry moved along to the back of the store, the closed door there against which he leaned one ear. Silence. Behind him a cat called, startled him. He turned, couldn't see the animal. Then there was silence again.

Ol' Henry rapped on the door with his fist, but not too hard.

Listening again, he heard movements inside. The sounds came closer. The door opened. The girl Lucy was limned in the doorway, bathed by moonlight. She wore a close-fitting shift and she carried a shotgun, the twin muzzles poking perilously close to the oldster's belly, and him with both hands away from his Colt, which was maybe for the best anyway.

The girl looked startled.

A shotgun in the hands of a fidgety female was not Ol' Henry's idea of a congenial meeting in the small hours. He said, 'Everything all right?'

'Of course. Why wouldn't it be? What do you want?'

Her voice was sharp, unusually so for her, this young female that the oldster had always thought of as completely inoffensive, meek even, a nonentity. Ol' Henry hadn't had a drink in what seemed a hell of a long time and that was what might have caused him to be fidgety, snappy, shotgun or no shotgun.

'Don't point that thing at me, gal,' he said.

She lowered the gun. He wondered at how quickly she'd gotten downstairs. Unless she slept down here of course: he wouldn't know about that. He went on: 'I was out takin' the air a while back and I saw two young fellers leave through this door kinda quiet-like. Mighty quiet-like.'

'Visitors,' said Lucy. 'They didn't want to disturb anybody.'

'Strangers.' It was half-statement, half-question. Did Ol' Henry know one of those younkers from way back? He still couldn't remember.

'Mysterious things have been happening around here lately—and seeing strangers in the night ...' The oldster let his sentence tail off.

And Lucy said, 'You don't have to worry. But thanks for being careful for us.'

'Makes no never-mind. How is your Uncle George anyway?' It seemed strange, referring to Twilight as 'Uncle George'.

'He's not too well. Touch of the croup I think.' She stepped aside. 'Come in for a bit.'

'I can't stop.' But, curious, he followed her.

Through the kitchen into another room. He had never been in back here before. Table, chairs, a few other items. And against a wall a wide sofa made up as a bed, tumbled clothes upon it. This was obviously where the girl slept.

Ahead was the door which obviously led

into the shop. But there was another door to which the girl crossed. Through the flimsy shift she wore and in the light of the moon through the uncurtained window Ol' Henry could see the shape of her and was surprised by the look of it.

She had always looked shapeless before in the dowdy clothes she wore at the counter. A plain girl. But a plain girl with a surprisingly voluptuous figure.

'Isn't it a beautiful night?' the oldster said lamely.

She didn't answer him, opened the second door, held it wide, made a beckoning action with her head. He went over to her.

'Listen,' she said.

Ol' Henry could hear Twilight snoring, sounding like a bull buffalo with nostril trouble.

'Have you had the doc to him?'

'No, but I'm going to if he isn't soundin' better in the morning.'

'So those two boys didn't see him?'

'They didn't come to see him. They came to see me. One of them's my cousin.'

Ol' Henry wondered, which one? He didn't ask.

'They were just passing through,' she said. 'Wanted to make it earlier but couldn't manage that. Just sat a while an' took coffee an' jawed.'

'Well, I better get back to the office. Sorry I bothered you.'

'That's all right, suh.' She was very polite now, but not as if addressing a customer.

A strange girl, Ol' Henry thought, as he left the place. He'd never thought of her like that before.

Twilight hadn't known that Lucy had had visitors this night. Did she have visitors like that, 'cousins', often down in her own little bivouac while the fat man slept like a grampus upstairs?

It was a thought to conjure with ...

Fourteen

She was a Westerner. She had always thought of herself, Western girl, through and through, and she still did.

When colleagues at her Eastern college had made snide remarks about her accent she had told them she was proud of it.

Ultimately, many of them had grown to like her for her humour and forthrightness: she had known this. Since returning home she had corresponded with a few of her colleagues back there, including another near-Westerner—from Chicago actually.

She would miss them. Some had promised to visit, but she knew that if they did not she would slowly forget them.

This was where she belonged, here in the wide spaces. This was where she would stay. Her home-coming had been a jamboree. Her father and his retainers had greeted her like a princess.

The usually taciturn and tough old rancher had been voluble and emotional. But not so her brother Glyn. She was not sure whether he was glad to see her back or not. Although she figured that he would back her at a pinch they had never been really close and he had referred to her in the past as 'Daddy's little girl'.

Still, he was older than her and remembered their mother, the woman their father had called 'faithless'. Maybe Glyn had been fonder of the woman than anybody had ever suspected whereas Irma barely remembered her.

Such thoughts! Now of all times!

Things had changed. Lately, so much. How awfully things had changed! And in such a short time it seemed—already her college days appeared to have been but a brief hiatus in time.

Things had fallen apart terribly, *terribly*.

Her father, a tough frontier businessman, had always looked out for her. He had been indulgent. She had been cared for, protected, *surrounded.*

But in the old days, in her childhood when there were not so many people in this wide, wild land, she had not needed so much protection.

At first she had gone out riding (side-saddle) with an escort. But later she had been allowed to ride astride—a fine cowgirl—alone in this peaceful territory that was watched over by the minions of Silas Deagle, monarch of all he surveyed.

On her rides later, but before college (she had had a tutor for a while) she had met Dack Simms and they had become firm friends.

She wondered where Dack was now.

Dack could look after himself!

But she should not have been riding alone at this time after hearing of the things that had been happening in this territory of late.

She had slipped away ...

What an arrogant fool she had been!

Now she was trussed like a turkey, with a stopper in her mouth. And she was deathly scared, all her strange thoughts blundering around in her head like frightened bats who had lost their faculties and sought to escape the dark.

The two men had left her for a while. She thought that one of them had gone away temporarily. But, if so, he was now back. She could hear low voices talking outside. And she was wondering what they meant to do with her.

While they were absent, or just the one gone and the other waiting and watching silently outside, she had struggled to free herself, but to no avail.

She had also been trying to figure out where she was.

She was pretty sure, yes, that she had the answer to that now.

The disused old line-hut at the outskirts of the Sunburst range on the sloping scrubland which overlooked the flat, barren, sprawling badlands where she had never ventured.

The old hut had at many times been the point of her return to base after a fairly long ride. It had been abandoned to the elements when she was just a sprig. The last time she saw it, it had been a ruin. Nobody came here now. It was not a salubrious place.

The two men had gagged her and tied her hands and feet but they had not blindfolded her. She lay on her side on a pile of straw which smelled with the sourness of age. Despite her position, the moonlight streamed in on to her face from huge gaps in the tumbledown structure that partially surrounded her.

She had her knees up, had tried to struggle while lying that way. She had not had much success—if any—but had stayed in that position as it was the most comfortable except for the tickling of the straw, the smell of it in her nostrils.

At first it had made her sneeze. But she did not heed it now. She did not know how long she had been here: it seemed a great time. The benign moonlight mocked her ...

She heard bootheels. There were still fragments of boards left in the line-hut which, like all Sunburst outhouses and suchlike, had been well and strongly built.

She saw one of the young men. The one she had thought was the least harmful of the two owlhooters. Handsome. Boyish-looking even.

But something in his face now. Something she did not like.

He bent over and quickly untied the rawhide at her ankles.

She saw his eyes.

She kicked out at him.

He drew back, laughing nastily, and she missed him.

Then her legs were pinned and he had his hands on her hips and was rolling her.

He was pushing her. Frantically, she jerked her torso upwards. She thought she heard sounds behind her attacker ...

She used her head, ramming it into his face as he loomed over her. Crying out, he was thrown backwards.

Her head hurt. But he was hurt more.

The violent action had in some way served to dislodge her gag, a sort of balled scarf, tied; she opened her mouth, but at first only a thin sound came out.

She tried again, straining her throat, her lungs. She swelled. The sound that issued then startled even her. She screamed. She screamed hard and long as if demented. The second young man was coming through what had once been the doorway of the old line-hut. He was shouting something but she did not hear.

The first young man lurched to his feet, his face bloodied, a gun in his fist. Suddenly it was like a play in which she was taking a part—and there seemed to be what sounded like horses' hooves backstage

... Like a playlet she had starred in back in college, though, really, it had been nothing like this.

She yelled. There was the louder sound of horses. Certainly not backstage. *From the front.* And she knew that her own horse, as well as the mounts belonging to the two kidnappers, had been put round back.

There was a shot! There was the smell of dust and gunsmoke. The handsome young kidnapper staggered and dropped his gun, twisted, fell down beside her, bloodied face, eyes staring sightlessly, no temper or lust in them now, just incomprehension. Then the boyish face settled and the eyes became glazed with the blankness of death.

The second man was already through the back, and out of her sight. But then there were other men—they were all around her ...

Fifteen

They had him on the long rope again, his feet barely touching the ground. He had passed out. He had been choking. He wasn't even doing that now and some of the boys were getting worried, their faces strained in the moonlight. Since they used the rope on him he hadn't been talking. Before that he'd been pretty voluble, for him. His voice had carried conviction. But Glyn Deagle had ignored this. And Glyn always had his own way: his old man was the only person who could override him.

A ranny said, 'We ought to let him down, Glyn. He can't tell us anything like that.'

'He's gonna die then,' said Glyn harshly.

Another man said, 'There's somebody coming,' ran to the edge of the glade, back. 'A bunch. The posse I think.'

'Let him down,' said Glyn and this was done.

He sprawled on the sward, the hemp coiled around him, the noose still at his throat.

There was moustached Sheriff Abel Codine and his deputies.

'Sweet Jesus,' a young deputy said. 'What's goin' on here?'

The sheriff and his chief deputy Bill Legwell got swiftly down from their horses, the younger man, who was leaner than the sheriff getting in first, bending over the man on the ground, who was beginning to cough wrenchingly.

Bill's face was aghast in the moonlight as he turned.

'It's Dack Simms.'

Codine confronted Glyn Deagle, said in a deep, threatening voice, 'Explain yourself.'

'He knows where Irma is an' he won't tell us,' stormed Glyn. 'We've got to make

149

him talk. There mightn't be much time. We've got to find Irma.' His voice shook. 'Take a good look at him.' He pointed to the man on the ground; his hand shook. 'Fancy gear. Twin guns. He's a pistoleer. He's been fooling all of us. I always thought there was something false about him. And he knew my sister better than either of 'em let on. She trusted him ...'

He was suddenly inarticulate, charged forward, swinging a boot. The sheriff caught his shoulder, spun him, threw him forcefully backwards so that he almost fell.

He straightened, looked for a moment as if he would go for his gun. 'Don't try it, bucko,' said Codine. And the younger man let his right hand fall.

Codine held him with an intense gaze, eyes shining in the moonlight. 'We found Irma. She's all right. Two of my boys have taken her back to the ranch. There were two men. We killed one of 'em. The other one got away. He came in this direction.

We thought you might have heard him makin' for the badlands.'

Glyn said, 'We didn't hear anything.'

None of his boys spoke. And the sheriff said thickly, 'No, you were too busy to hear anything, weren't you?'

Dack Simms had been helped to his feet, was leaning against the tree which, if the posse hadn't turned up, could have been the means of his death. Nobody was sure whether Glyn Deagle would have carried out his threat or not.

Dack wasn't talking, wasn't coughing now. He had his hand up to his throat and his gaze was fixed on Glyn and the sheriff who stood a little away from the rest. Dack's hands had been tied. Now they were loose, having been cut by a deputy with a huge jack-knife.

As a last mockery Glyn Deagle had left the captured man's twin pearl-handled Colts in their holsters as they strung him up, his toes pointed: had he kicked he would have choked himself.

As the deputies lifted the choking man from the ground Deputy Bill Legwell had taken his guns, which seemed to be the sensible thing to do—him with his hands free now an' all, Bill had reflected. One quick savage move and this once peaceful glade could turn into a sort of bloodbath.

Dack was waiting. Massaging his wrists. Massaging his throat gently. He hadn't spoken.

Sheriff Codine said, 'We've got the man we shot out here. We want you to look at him. None of us have seen him before, but one of you boys might've, being part of the ranch an' seeing waddies an' drifters an' the like.' The implication was obvious. The big man led the way out of the glade.

At first the Sunburst men said they hadn't seen the man before, looped over the back of a horse, his head lifted by his hair in the hands of a deputy, the young handsome face lit by the moonlight. 'He looks kinda peaceful now,' said the deputy who held a hank of hair. Then, as if on an afterthought, one of the cowboys spoke up.

'I saw him earlier tonight just after dark. By the ranch. Looked as if he was comin' from the ranch. Dunno whether he saw me or not, gave no sign. I figured mebbe he'd been asking for a job, mebbe was even about to start one in the mornin' an' was ridin' into town to celebrate.'

The sheriff asked, 'Anybody else near?'

'Nobody.'

More questions. Nobody else had spotted this man at the ranch it seemed. Or, if they had, they weren't letting on.

The sheriff said, 'The other bozo is to hell an' gone by now. We'll go back to the ranch, see if Miss Irma can tell us anything.'

During the ride the man who had always called himself Dack Simms (maybe it was his own name after all, his companions might have opined) since he'd been in the Sandela Strip territory, didn't say a word on the ride to the Sunburst Ranch. There wasn't much talking from anybody. The ranchmen in particular were as silent as so many mutes, even Glyn, though he rode upright in the saddle with his usual arrogant look on his face.

Everybody it seemed had a lot of cogitating to do. Some would wonder what Dack Simms would have to do to Glyn Deagle. The man would have to do something. He had a weal on his neck that would remind him of Glyn and his boys for some time to come.

Glyn had called him 'a pistoleer'. But Glyn himself was by way of being a pistoleer also, as he had amply demonstrated at back of the ranch in shooting contests from time to time.

But Glyn had never been known to kill a man with his gun, though he had wounded one half-drunken waddie who'd thrown down on him one night in town.

Yeh, he was fast, was Glyn.

But Dack still didn't have his guns.

And Sheriff Codine was riding close to Glyn, keeping an eye on him. Some of the posse-members who disliked the ranch son and his high-and-mighty ways might have thought that the sheriff was being easy on him; but nobody said so.

They reached the ranch. There was activity. Lights. Silas Deagle came out on the porch. Everybody wanted to know how Irma was. Silas said she was all right. She was in her bed. Her father had insisted that she rest.

He had news for everybody.

A folded paper had been found beneath a mug on the cookhouse table. Somebody must have slipped through the back door when the cook, old Jules, had been in another part of the house: it was probably when he was serving his 'lovely favourite' as he called his 'Miss Irma', with some hot soup.

Silas handed the note to the sheriff, saying, 'Nobody was spotted.'

Codine said, 'I think somebody was, by

one of your men. We caught one of those two, shot him ...'

'Yes, your two boys told me. They're in the kitchen having some chow.'

'Pity he was completely deaded,' the sheriff said, almost jovially. 'He couldn't tell us anything. And the other one got away. We have other things to report, I'm mighty sorry to say.'

'What?'

'I'll tell you. But first I will read this note aloud if you don't mind.'

'All right.'

Codine had a deep, sonorous voice, making the banal words sound menacing.

WE HAVE YOUR DAUGHTER. WE WANT FIVE THOUSAND DOLLARS. DO NOT TRY AND DOUBLECROSS US OR SHE WILL DIE. FURTHER INSTRUCTIONS WILL FOLLOW.

Silas had sent his men away, all except his son. The two Deagles were in the spacious sitting-room with the sheriff and his men and the silent Dack Simms who now had his bandanna knotted, not too tightly, around his throat.

There were gasps from some of the men. One deputy said, 'They could've asked for more. I guess they weren't being too greedy.'

Tasteless maybe. Still, the Deagles weren't exactly the prime favourites of the folks of Sandela.

Codine waved the note, said, 'It's quite literate. Block letters. Seems a shaky hand though. Hard to trace.'

One of the men said, 'They were young, those two. Nothing shaky about them.'

'They maybe couldn't write anyway,' said somebody else.

'Maybe it was written that way, shaky an' all, to fool us,' the sheriff said. 'Well, you've got your girl back, Silas, so I don't guess there'll be any further instructions, any follow-up. Whether we will be able to catch that other young jasper, however, is a question I can't answer right now. But we'll do our best.'

The big man turned away, said a few quiet words to Deputy Bill Legwell. Bill moved. He went behind Glyn Deagle. There was a sharp metallic click. Bill, although because of his recent wound couldn't move quite as fast as he usually did, had managed to grab the Deagle son's arms, jerk them around his back, fasten handcuffs to his wrists.

Taken completely by surprise Glyn could only make a shocked sound; and 'Why ...?'

Codine cut in on that, turning to face the father once more. 'I'm taking your son in for attempted murder, Silas. I ought to take some of your boys too. But they'll keep. I'll need 'em as witnesses I guess.'

'What?'

But the sheriff went on remorselessly, half-turning, 'Take him out, boys. I'll explain to his father. It won't take long. Wait. You too, Dack.'

Dack Simms merely nodded his head.

Codine watched them go, then turned again to Silas who looked bemused, unusual for him. 'It's for your son's protection as well. I think Simms aims to kill him. And I wouldn't blame him for that.'

Silas opened his mouth again. 'What?'

Codine bulled on, told the story bluntly, succinctly.

Sixteen

A head lifted again by a hank of hair.

Ol' Henry stooping, looking into a dead face.

'Yeh, I've seen him before. Earlier. Comin' outa the back door o' Twilight's place. Him an' another young feller. Longfaced, dark, mean-lookin', maybe some Injun in him. Never see'd this one before tonight, but I had seen the other one, sure o' that, but can't remember where or when—or who, y'know.'

'The other one got away,' said Sheriff Codine.

The dead head was lowered and Ol' Henry turned away, was looking at Deputy Legwell. 'You all right, son? I said you shouldn't have gone along with this bunch. You look kinda peaked.'

'I'm all right.'

'You ain't,' said Abe Codine. 'Henry's right. You go along to the doc's place. You too, Dack.'

'Oh, all right. Come on, Dack.'

The two moved away. Glyn Deagle, expostulating loudly now, had been put in a cell. The posse had split up. No more riding tonight. Everybody badly needed some shut-eye. It would soon be morning. This would be a night to remember all right.

Strangely, there'd been no more rustling or robbing. But this last go-down had beat all. Not bad results though, after all. A girl saved. A man almost hanged. But only *almost*. A kidnapper dead. Another one to hell and gone.

But maybe Ol' Henry would remember him—and that would help. Unless the old 'un had been having drunken pipe-dreams—wouldn't be the first time.

He'd seemed sober as a sleeping judge, however.

In the office Abe Codine said, 'You stay here, Henry. I'm going next door to see the fat man.'

'They'll be asleep.'

'I'll wake 'em up.'

Glyn Deagle was yelling again from his cell. As Codine passed through the back door he heard Henry tell the prisoner to stow it or he'd get watered down by the bucketful. Henry had had that treatment himself when he'd been drunk and obstreperous and noisy. It worked like a luck-charm on a whore's ankle, made a man breathless.

His name was Nick Sintaine. He was a killer, a robber, a hard-rider. There was a price on his head in other places but he wasn't known in the Sandela Strip country.

His horse was lathered and lurching when they reached the hideout, a freak place. In the badlands but near a tiny spring which nurtured grass and small trees around it.

Folks crossing the badlands towards the border kept to the beaten track, frightened of losing themselves, ultimately losing a life.

From the narrow trail—you needed a good, strong horse and plenty of water—meagre as it was, the hiding place, the vegetation, the spring could not be seen.

And there the boys had waited impatiently. They hadn't done any night-riding since the raid on Sandela, had had orders not to do so. And here now was Sintaine, alone, and vociferously they wanted to know why. Then 'Hold it' one man thundered.

His name was Halo, just that, nobody knew why. He was Mexican and very big, more muscle than fat, and with the temper of a bloated sidewinder. He wasn't the big boss. But he was the leader now, a better fighter with fists and weapons than even the new arrival Nick Sintaine. And it was to him directly that Nick told his story.

'I never was in favour o' that thing from the start,' Halo said. 'It ain't my kind o' business.'

There were murmurs: the consensus seemed to be with him on that last pronouncement. And Sintaine, after his talking, was plumb worn out. 'Ain't there any coffee?' he demanded plaintively.

'Big goddamn kidnapper,' sneered Halo. 'Did you have that filly, Nick?'

'Didn't bother. Too fancy for me. Leo tried, though.' Nick gave a nervously explosive guffaw, startling everybody. 'An' look what happened to him.'

'Somebody else comin',' said the look-out.

One man. Easily recognizable. A jackal. A jackal of a messenger with fraught news. An oddjob man from town who worked with all kinds of folk. Called Slopey because of his lopsided gait from a childhood accident he wasn't nearly so stupid and unknowing as the townies thought him to be and had many secret sidelines. His occupation with the border bunch was one of the best: he was the go-between that the big boss needed.

'They got young Glyn,' he blurted out. 'He's in jail.'

He told a garbled story and, when he had finished, big Halo said, 'I allus figured that proud turkey-cock bastard'd go off half-cocked sooner or later. Nick an' Leo had his sister f'Chrissakes. It was a bad scheme. You cain't play two ends agin the middle like that. We've got to get that smart, talky bastard outa that cell before he blows.'

'The boss ain't gonna like you doin' that on your lonesome,' said Slopey.

'I've got these boys behind me.'

There were murmurs of assent. 'And you're comin' in with us,' said Halo.

'I don't think ...' Slopey's sentence tailed off.

He looked around him, squinty eyes shining in the moonlight. He was surrounded.

Bill Legwell's wound had burst open again, and the doc had to fix it, called the young deputy an idiot for going out with the posse. Bill was too beat to argue with him, maybe agreed with the irascible medico now, went home to his bed the way he was told.

Not so Dack Simms. The taciturn man was fairly fit. He hadn't actually been beaten, only half-hanged. He had a ropeburn on his neck. He had his twin guns back. Sheriff Codine had opined that Simms wasn't the sort to shoot a man while he lay in a cell. So, for the time being, Glyn Deagle was safe in his incarceration than he would be anyplace else.

Dack went back to the law office. The sheriff was out. Ol' Henry was dozing in the sheriff's armchair, had the door locked. Roused, he let Dack in.

The sheriff came back, said, 'The girl told me what she told you, Henry, that those two boys called on her. She said one of 'em was her cousin.'

'She didn't tell me that.' But had she? The old man couldn't remember. His mind had been bedevilled by other things since his visit to the neighbours.

Dack looked from one to the other of the two older men but didn't say anything until the sheriff had explained things, though it wasn't much of an explanation, not yet. Codine added that Twilight had been snoring and the girl Lucy had said she thought the fat man was sick with croup.

'I think she said that to me,' put in Ol' Henry. But had she?

Dack said, 'I've always thought that that fat, greedy cuss ain't exactly what he seems.'

'He is kind of a fat dark horse I guess,' said Codine. 'Maybe I ought to go visit him again, wake him up, croup or no croup.'

But Glyn Deagle was yelling again. Dack looked in the direction of the cell-block, didn't move, said, 'The way he acted. Glyn. Peculiar. Crazy. As if the hanging, the trying to make me talk like he said, was just play-acting and he wanted to shut my mouth for good anyway. As if he thought I knew somep'n I shouldn't, somep'n of a danger to him. I think he has somep'n to do with what's been happenin' in this territory recently.'

'Not with the kidnapping of his own sister, surely,' said the sheriff.

'Who knows what a crazy man will do? Maybe the kidnapping of his sister was a separate thing.'

'Rustling his own father's stock ...'

'Not a lot, you said so yourself as I remember. That'd draw suspicion away from the Sunburst, wouldn't it?'

Codine looked doubtful but said, 'Glyn and his old man never got on too well, I know that. Silas always doted on Irma. He didn't marry again ...'

Ol' Henry interrupted, more wildly than was his custom. 'I've got it!'

The sheriff demanded, 'What's the matter with you?'

'The young feller I saw comin' outa Twilight's back door, one o' them two, the pard of the one who you brought back good an' deaded, I remember who the other one was. It just come to me.'

He was out of breath. The other two looked at him silently. Then he went on, 'His name's Nick Sintaine, Killer. An' other things, price on his head. I see'd him kill a man back in Austin some years ago. I was visitin' my old aunt afore she died. Sintaine was just a sprig then makin' a rep for himself, got in an argument with a local gunny an' they faced each other in the street. The other man lost. Straight-up fight. Sintaine won fairly. Mighty damn' fast. It was afterwards I heard of Sintaine again, mixed in some pretty raw things.'

'Wait,' said Codine. 'I think I've got a dodger.' He rummaged in his desk. 'Yeh, here it is. No picture. But a good description.' He read it out.

'That's him all right,' crowed Ol' Henry. 'I knew I'd place 'im sooner or later.'

Back in his cell Glyn Deagle had become quiet.

It was as if he'd been listening to the suddenly loud voices.

Seventeen

Sheriff Abel Codine reflected, so many folks who were not exactly as they seemed—or far from it. But wasn't that the way of the West? He had secrets himself—who didn't? He told himself that he had never been completely fooled by the taciturn 'sodbuster' who called himself Dack Simms.

But Dack, whatever he'd been before—a hired gun; an owlhooter—was on the right side now, even if he had in a sense been forced into that, and almost hanged in the process.

So, right now, Abe didn't want to find out all about Dack.

But he sure as hell wanted to find out more about fat Twilight and his 'niece' Lucy. He made his second visit there as the dawn approached. And Dack Simms came along with him while Ol' Henry, with both doors locked, awaited returning signal-knocks at the jailhouse.

The back door of the stores was locked. Codine knocked on it with his fist. There was no reply, no sound from inside. The sheriff hammered. Nothing happened.

'I'm gonna wake all the neighbours.' The sheriff put his ear to the door. 'Nothing. Maybe they're in the shop.'

'It's early for that, ain't it?' said Dack. 'But if you stay here I'll go an' check.'

Up an alley, round a corner. The shop was shuttered and blind. His eyes close to the window, he could only see the clutter inside, no movement. He retraced his steps. Shook his head.

'T'aint right,' said the sheriff. 'I'm gonna bust the door in.'

This was quickly done. The sounds died and inside there was silence and nobody appeared to remonstrate with them.

They searched the place.

The girl's cot was neatly made. Upstairs, Twilight's bedclothes were rumbled, thrown back. Everything was empty.

'I guess he got over his croup,' said Codine sardonically.

'Can the fat freak ride?' Dack asked.

'He's got a gig with two fast trotters. Let's get down to the livery stable.'

The hostler was awakened from his bed, grumbled, 'You're the second folks this mornin'. I only just got to sleep again.'

'Was it Twilight and the girl?'

'Yes.'

'Which way did they go?'

'I didn't watch 'em.'

They went to the edge of town, didn't see anybody. Which way? A few folks were beginning to stir themselves, curtains moving, faces from windows, a man with a dog. The man hadn't heard any hoofbeats, wheels. The dog would've barked; hadn't.

The other side of town. Nothing.

'I should've bearded that fat bastard in his den,' snorted the sheriff. 'I guess he was playing possum. Snores an' all. An' the girl was telling lies.'

'You couldn't know. If Ol' Henry hadn't remembered that one o' the visitors was a noted killer ...'

'Hell, we'd got the other one, hadn't we?'

They were back in town when they were made aware of the approaching horsemen in the busy early-morning light. A large bunch, unrecognizable, coming fast, something ominous about the look of them.

Odd-job man Slopey falling from a horse and running frantically away from them, shouting, waving his arms.

A single shot. And Slopey falling, rolling, coming to a stop in the street, twitching, lying still.

'They seem to be making for the jail,' the sheriff yelled.

The two men took to the sidewalk, ran, crouching low. The thunder of hooves rose as the bunch came on.

The border bunch?

They were awakening a somnolent town to shocking awareness, fumbling for answers, defence, retaliation.

Ol' Henry had the front door of the jailhouse open, his rifle in his fists. He came out on to the sidewalk and dropped on one knee, levelled quickly, fired off two shots, swivelling the gun slightly after the first one, which didn't hit anything. But the other one did, fetching a man off his horse, though, limping, he made shelter.

A rifle was more accurate than a handgun. After the killing of Slopey, lying like a throwaway bundle on the edge of the street, the bunch seemed to be just making havoc, noise. A lot of the populace was still indoors, and scrabbling for weapons no doubt. But most of them were peaceable folk, not gunhawks and, for a time, the bunch had them buffaloed.

Now, however, the sheriff and his new deputy, Dack Simms, were in the jailhouse with the now-retreating old jailer. They had left a gap in the door and broken a window, which the bunch would've probably done for them anyway. But now they were under fire and, though trying not to get unhorsed, were taking cover themselves.

Their leader, Halo, backed by his *compadre*, Nick Sintaine, was as cunning and devilish as any of them, and more so than most. He had sent men on foot round to the back of the jail. Three *pistoleros*, matching the three inside their bulwark, which soon ceased to be anything of that kind.

The lock of the back door was blown off with a blast from a sawn-off shotgun. Sheriff Codine, while turning, yelled at Henry to watch the front door which the old man had chosen for his spot. The snap of the oldster's trusty old rifle, the muzzle pointing out at the street, was answer enough.

Dack Simms was turning, moving sideways at the same time, making a wider gap between himself and Abe Codine.

The three men came in past the cell-block and one of them passed a Colt revolver through the bars to Glyn Deagle.

There was one point that the would-be rescuers had overlooked however; a small one, but a telling one. When they had moved out back they hadn't seen a soul in the not yet clear morning light, not even a half-dressed figure crossing to a privy. So, at the door, they hadn't watched their backs.

Deputy Bill Legwell, after returning from his hard ride with the posse, had under-standably discovered that his wound was playing him up, hadn't needed much urging from his chief to go to bed and rest. But, keyed-up, he hadn't slept very well.

He was wideawake when he heard the hoofbeats, then the single shot which killed jackal Slopey, although right then Bill hadn't been aware of the little go-between's abrupt demise.

Bill jumped out of bed, winced, began to get dressed. His erratic movements roused his mother, Beth, in the next room, although she had an idea that something else had disturbed her before that. And now she was alarmed. She put on slippers and a robe and went out on to the landing. Bill came out of his room and almost charged into her.

'There's trouble,' he said. 'You get the rifle and stay by the front window downstairs but don't show yourself. Don't move until I get back, unless you have to.'

He was all lawman now, and she reacted without comment on his orders, merely saying, 'All right.' She couldn't stop him, could only add, when downstairs, 'Take care, son', as he left. And, as that was the quickest way to the jailhouse from the frame house, he went along the backs of town.

There was more shooting from in front. Then the boom of shotgun from the back.

And then Bill was in sight of the back of the jail and he saw the three men go through the door and, favouring his wounded side, he ran, hoppity-skip, his gun in his hand.

The men didn't see him. Then he was through the back door in their wake, and they didn't hear him either: he had put on stout moccasins instead of his riding boots.

They were making enough noise themselves now and, in a split second, all hell would break loose.

Eighteen

Big Halo, leaving his men to get on with their depredations, their jail-attack, broke into Twilight's store and went right through it. He even called, though not too loudly. Gunfire from other sources was intermittent. Halo, his gun in his hand, had no need to use the weapon.

The upstairs and downstairs of the stores was empty of humankind—and Twilight had never kept a cat or dog. The fat man and the girl, Lucy, had vanished—and Halo was mighty sure that they had taken what they needed with them.

His temper rising to a killing fury, the big man dashed from the place but then had to take cover again immediately. The jasper who was using a rifle from the jailhouse door was some shooter.

The gunfire was still intermittent but growing.

The three outlaws in the jailhouse were facing two of their own kind, though the defenders were on a different side of the fence, if you could put it that way. And a third man on that side, a fiery-looking oldster, was turning away from the door with rifle uplifted in his paws.

Momentarily, the defenders had the advantage. With the blast from the destroyed back door they had been warned of the sneak attack which, suddenly, wasn't a sneak attack any more.

The defenders reacted with caginess. The sheriff was half-covered by his big desk. His partner was crouched more towards the wall, becoming almost part of a tall many-pronged coat-rack which held various items of outdoor clobber, left there to dry after the recent rains.

The three defenders opened up almost simultaneously and the office was filled with a cacophony of hideous, blattering noise and a pall of black gunsmoke which stung the nostrils and eyes as much as the gunfire stunned the ears.

In the enclosed space the guns in the hands of men who were professionals at what they did were pretty accurate. But the Henry rifle in the hands of the oldster to whom it had lent a nickname, though this weapon was further away from the attackers than were the handguns, was the most effective.

An attacker cried out in agony and fell backwards, his gun parabolling from his hand. He lay still. But, at the same time, Ol' Henry, who had no cover, was hit in the leg, which gave way beneath him. The minor wound saved his bacon, for another slug buzzed harmlessly over his head which was much lower than it had been before.

Neither Abe nor Dack were hit by the first barrage and they were both down on one knee and triggering methodically. Another attacker caught a slug which burned his neck but didn't bring him down. The third man escaped hurt, was, like the two men who faced him, down on one knee.

There was a short breath of a pause in the office as men peered at each other through the fog of gunsmoke.

Shots came from the cell-block.

Out of the cell and gun in hand with which he had blown the lock, Glyn Deagle was in the passage and about to follow his rescuers. He hesitated though, turning to look towards the back door as if quickly debating making a run for it in that direction.

He got a surprise.

Bill Legwell was facing him, gun in hand.

Guns rising.

They fired almost simultaneously.

But Bill had the slight edge.

Glyn screamed with shock and pain as a single bullet bored into his chest and smashed him back along the passage and against the wall. He slid down this slowly, the light flaring in his eyes and then dying completely.

His shot had missed its mark by a small fraction, the slug thudding into the door at Bill Legwell's back.

In the office the remaining two men had had enough. Leaving their dead comrade on the floor of the office, they turned to make their escape the way they'd come in. One of them was unharmed, the other's neck had begun to trickle blood.

In their headlong flight the two outlaws almost knocked Deputy Legwell sprawling. Twisted against the wall beside the open doorway which led in to the office, Bill only glimpsed retreating backs, and they disappeared before he could get a shot at them.

As Bill rose, Dack Simms came into the passage, looked startled, asked, 'You all right?'

'Fine.' Bill jerked a thumb. 'But he isn't.'

Dack didn't argue, went over to Glyn

against the wall, bent, paused, then said in a strangely high-pitched voice, 'No, by all that's holy, there's still a breath of life in him.'

'Let's get out of here,' Halo had suddenly exclaimed, shouted even. Some of the boys were surprised. They wanted 'pickings' from this damn' town.

But the townsfolk had already suffered hurt and pillage from this bunch. They weren't sure that it was the same bunch, the 'border bunch' as they'd dubbed them—but they sure as hell had had their bellyful of this kind of thing, on top of all the recent mysterious happenings.

They were awake now, the townies, and they were at their windows and doors. Some of them were even on the streets, armed—everybody had a weapon of some kind—lying sort of doggo.

Halo didn't tell anybody that Twilight and Lucy had fled the nest. He had an idea, however, where they would be making for.

Halo had had the news about the gutshot Glyn Deagle—even if he was still alive he certainly wouldn't be able to ride. The two boys who had escaped from the jailhouse, leaving the third man dead behind them in the office, had had enough of a glance at Deagle to be sure that he was pretty far gone.

Even if he survived—and talked—the information he could give to the law would be little help to them now, with the kidnapped girl escaped, and Twilight and Lucy having done a disappearing act.

The thing was, Halo decided, to get after Twilight as soon as possible was the best, and maybe the only bet. Or, apart from what the boys and he had shared between themselves so far, there would be little else. As for any boodle they could get from this town: that wasn't worth wasting time with now.

Halo led his men out at a gallop.

Not an uninterrupted one, however.

The damn' townies seemed to have suddenly got together a bunch of fire-crackers and were setting them off almost simultaneously.

Nineteen

Dark, fox-faced Nick Sintaine had stuck as close to Halo as a burr on a burro's butt. Halo didn't like the man, didn't trust him, didn't send him anyplace particular in case he went hog-wild. Maybe Sintaine was better where Halo could keep an eye on him.

Things weren't going as Halo had planned, not nearly. Lately, in fact, nothing seemed to be going as planned, though Halo hadn't exactly been in on the original planning, or what he thought of as the 'extra'. Halo, somewhat of a superstitious turn of mind as he was, thought it was that 'extra' which he sort of brought about a jinx against the whole proceedings.

The big man had been a thief ever since he was a tad, and a killer not long after that: he was a seasoned *comanchero*. He drew no line on rustling, the setting of fires, the pillaging and sacking of a town: it was all meat to his black soul.

But, he told himself, he didn't make war on women. He hadn't known at first about the kidnapping of the Deagle girl, the one they called Irma. Pickings had been pretty good anyway. And the snatching of a daughter of the most powerful man in the Sandela Strip was like to blow up a storm.

Halo was sneakingly glad that that particular plan had gone haywire, that one of the kidnappers had gotten his comeuppance: pity Sintaine hadn't similarly: the bastard was too smart for his own damn' good.

Maybe I'll finish him myself, Halo thought, after he's outlived his usefulness.

Past the neck of his own horse Halo looked at Sintaine, who was just a mite ahead of him, pushing his own galloping mount.

They kept their heads down. There was gunfire all around them in the red of the dawning sun.

The townies seemed to have gone hog-wild!

Halo saw Sintaine's horse hit, its legs buckling. Sintaine was thrown from the saddle, seemed momentarily to disappear in a haze of dust and gunsmoke.

He appeared again like a ghost out of a mist and by then Halo was almost past him, glancing at him. Sintaine was on his feet again but staggering, looking stunned, didn't seem to spot Halo and his mount. Two men and one horse like creatures in a mist, a dead horse behind them, disappearing.

Then another figure, on foot, a shirt-sleeved, bearded man with a shotgun which pointed at Sintaine like a steel rod and exploded with noise and fire and smoke.

The charge drove Sintaine backwards, the gun he'd drawn parabolling redly in the dusty sun. Sintaine's legs kicked up and he almost cartwheeled and his head hit the rutted ground very hard. He was spread like a dead frog, and still.

Halo took a sideways shot at the bearded man and missed. I'm outa here, he thought, and urged his horse to even greater speed.

He saw one of his men go ass over heels from the saddle, his face streaming with blood. The man wobbled after the horse, maybe said something: who could hear anything with all the din that was going on? Well, maybe the horse heard, hesitated, even looked back. And his rider was able to climb back into the saddle.

Passing him, Halo yelled, 'You all right, Colley?'

'Yeh, just a crease.' Then the wild younker called Colley was riding side by side with his chief as they hit the edge of town.

A handsome woman with a rifle was leaning from the window of a frame house and taking potshots with a rifle. She had already winged a bandit who had tried to take shelter on her porch because his horse had gone lame.

The man, a bullet in his arm, had been picked up by one of his *compadres:* they rode two in a saddle as they escaped.

Beth Legwell, mother of Deputy Bill and light-o'-life of Marshal Abel Codine, was giving a good account of herself Nobody else tried for her. The bandits streamed away.

'We goin' back to the hideout?' a man asked Halo.

'Nope, that's out for now. We're goin' someplace else.'

There hadn't been any fatalities in town, and nothing that the doc couldn't fix. There'd been minor pilferings but nothing anywhere near the boodle that was taken on the previous occasion that the border bunch hit the town.

Actually, it seemed that they had visited for another purpose this time and things had not gone at all as they had expected. So now a posse would have to be got together.

Twenty

Bill and Ol' Henry had joined Dack Simms and Sheriff Codine in the cell-block but kept themselves in the background.

Dack and Abe were still bending over Glyn Deagle who, miraculously, still had a breath of life in him.

Bill and Henry heard Dack say, 'He's trying to talk.'

Dack, on one knee, bent closer to the dying man. Had Glyn asked a question? Was he asking some kind of forgiveness for something? Bill and Henry couldn't hear anything. The sheriff bent closer beside Dack. It was as if the two of them were breathing life into Glyn as long as they could.

'Twilight and the girl have gone, Glyn. Do you know where they have gone?' That was Dack's question.

Glyn was making strange sounds.

Bill and Henry, as one man, moved closer.

A word from dying lips. 'Ghost ...'

'*Ghost* ...' The whisper died. Glyn Deagle relaxed.

'He's dead,' Abe Codine said.

'What was he sayin?' Dack said. 'What was he trying to say? I heard one word. Sounded like ghost.'

'Yeh, I heard ghost. What did he mean?' Both men straightened themselves.

Behind them Ol' Henry said, 'There's a ghost town near the border. It was still there last time I was in that direction which ain't been more'n a year ago I guess. I don't know what it was called, even if it ever had a name. Nothing there. No folks or animals I mean. Hell, a real ghost town. Could still be some of it left. It's the kind of place that border scum would be likely to make for, ain't it—quick getaway?'

'I think I heard o' that,' said the sheriff.

'Didn't ever see it though.'

'I might've heard,' said Deputy Bill. 'But I ain't ever been that way, I don't think.'

They were all looking at Dack. It was his turn.

He seemed to be deep in thought, came out of it with deliberate slowness as if he hadn't quite made up his mind. He said, 'I think I know where you mean. I think I've been there ... If it's the same place.'

His voice died. He was thinking again. He was away from the three other men, *far away*. A name was in his mind, a phrase.

Three words.

Dale Consarn gunfighter.

A young man, little more than a boy, who had thought he was the very fastest, the fastest ever, much faster than the fastest. And in a lonely town empty of people he had tried to prove that he was the fastest. If only to prove it to himself. If only ...

But he hadn't proved it, and he had died.

Maybe his ghost still walked there in that lonely place where the wind blew over his grave ...

Twenty-One

It wasn't a big posse. Just the sheriff and his deputy, and Dack Simms and, this time, Ol' Henry, another oldster being left to look after the jailhouse. Plus a lot of alert townsfolk who didn't think the border bunch aimed to come back, but half-hoped that they would.

The posse was made up with three more youngish carefully picked gun-toters, so there was seven in all. Abe Codine had figured that was plenty: he didn't want any of 'em getting in each other's way, shooting each other in the brisket.

Hell, he hoped that they were on the right trail and that, at the end of it, there would be something that they could do more than sit in the saddles and look at a pesky ghost town which was empty—or just gone. *Gone* to the wind and the dust.

He rode next to Dack Simms and, at one time, reached into his vest pocket and took out a folded form and handed it to Dack saying, 'I meant to show you this before but it slipped my mind, what with everything that was happening an' all. It's a bill o' sale I picked up in Twilight's stores when I was in there. Young Lucy did all Twilight's writin' an' figurin' an' I reckon she made that out. Does that printin' look familiar to you?'

Bobbing in the saddle, Dack looked at the missive. Then he said, 'It looks like the printing that was on the ransom note ol' Silas Deagle got.'

'That's what I thought. And I've seen Lucy's printing before. Maybe she couldn't write any other way. Y'know, Dack, though I didn't say so at the time, I thought the wordin' on that ransom note looked kinda familiar. I guess I figured I was imagining things, kinda wishful thinkin', y'know.'

'Yeh. But I ain't ever seen Lucy's hand

before so I'm a sort of independent judge, ain't I? And, Abe, I think you're right—Lucy penned this and the ransom note.' Dack handed the bill back to the sheriff who tucked it into his pocket and patted it as if for safety.

The hooves ate up the miles. 'Won't be long now,' said Ol' Henry They hadn't seen a living soul, animal or human. The sun was hot and the air was still. The dust puffed, and ahead was a veil of heat-haze which fluctuated in a ghostly way.

'I hope we ain't on no wild goose chase,' said one of the youngish deputies.

'Don't look forward to Perdition, son,' said Ol' Henry. 'An' keep your powder dry.'

Lucy was supposed to be on look-out on the edge of town, but she was very tired and she went to sleep.

In recent times her life had gone much awry. She had been carried along willy-nilly and, a girl who always wanted to do what was expected of her, she had played her part as usual, the inoffensive stores girl. And, as usual, she had done what Twilight had wanted her to do.

She knew that the fat man carried a great hate in his heart. A hate for old friends and acquaintances in the Sandela Strip who had done so much better than he had. For Silas Deagle for one, and for all that Silas stood for. The fat man and Silas had come to the Strip at about the same time, and even been friends of a sort or, at least, friendly rivals.

Lucy had seen old tin-types—very early ones—of the two men as they had been in those far-off days. Twilight had been the bigger of the two but with no fat on him. He had not been called Twilight then.

He would never admit that it was his sloth and his greedy appetite that had made him what he was now.

His greed had never left him. He was like a fat spider spinning a web.

He was the one behind the border

bunch. The one they called the boss. The big man called Halo had taken his orders from Twilight, as had Nick Sintaine and his partner, the one called Leo.

But Twilight had begun to play both ends against the middle, had began to weave a more tangled web. Glyn Deagle, who had always hated his own father, had become an ally and it was from Glyn that Twilight had got news of cattle herds and what went on in business affairs in town. The rustling, the burning, the robbing and killing. Even, on Glyn's volition, a-picking at the Sunburst herds so suspicion would not look that way.

Twilight's long-standing envy of Silas Deagle, Twilight's hate, had driven the fat man to this. And to more! To the kidnapping of Irma Deagle at the hands of Nick and his partner, something Glyn hadn't known about until the last minute, though he had tried to cover up with accusations well away from the purlieu of fat Twilight, the stores in Sandela town.

Lucy had penned the ransom note because Twilight had told her to do so. She would not admit to herself that she was as full of envy as the fat man was, though she didn't have his greed, his miserly hiding away of crooked funds which soon, he thought, would make him a rich man looked up to in new lands.

They would have to move soon, he had said, go where nobody would find them and live off the fat of the land.

But the girl had not expected to be dragged from her bed in the dead of night, to be made to run like a thief, to be taken to a place that seemed little more than a large ruined graveyard ...

She was awakened from what had seemed like a nightmare and a figure that seemed huge and menacing was looming over her.

Twenty-Two

'Get up, girl,' a voice said.

She recognized those gruff tones, began to recognize the big face from which the voice had issued. Shading her eyes with her hands and squinting upwards, she made sure. 'Halo,' she said. She had always liked Halo. He had always been very polite to her.

He even caught her by her elbow now, to help her to her feet.

She saw the other men behind him, recognized some of them.

'Lead me to the fat man, honey,' Halo said. She didn't think he'd ever called her 'honey' before. She knew she had to do what he had asked.

She shouldn't have gone to sleep. But it was too late now.

'The back way,' Halo said, as they approached the broken-down house where Twilight sat, was maybe sleeping too, Lucy reflected.

The men had left their horses way back with one of their number to watch over them. They had moved spread out, choosing places to walk where there were no remnants of splintered boardwalk, nothing which they could stumble over. They walked catlike, wary, judging every movement they made, that any of their comrades in sight made also.

They waited outside, ringing the place but keeping out of sight as Lucy and Halo went round the back of the ruined house.

Glassless windows gaped at them. The back door sagged off its hinges and wild vegetation had crept its way into the kitchen.

Lucy knew that the upstairs of the place had virtually fallen in upon themselves and upon parts of the ground floor. There was a rickety, broken staircase that didn't seem to lead anywhere.

She had left Twilight sitting in an armchair with busted stuffing. From there he could watch the windows and the open doors at the front of the house; and the crooked stairs angled off to the left of him. He had obviously figured that somebody might try to get at him that way—though it hardly seemed likely.

The hot sun was on the necks of the big, catfooted man and the small, tripping girl.

'If he's good I'm not gonna hurt him,' the big man said softly. 'I'm only gonna take the money he ran out with 'cos some of it belongs to me an' my men, you know that, don't you?'

She nodded her head, and he went on, 'Call out to him softly. Tell 'im you're comin' in.'

Her voice was like a breeze. 'Uncle—I'm comin' in.'

Twilight's phlegm-laden tones answered.

'C'mon then, girl.'

Halo moved through the kitchen door ahead of Lucy and drew his gun.

Lucy realized that if Twilight didn't turn his armchair round he would be backing on Halo when the big man entered the room where the fat man sat, waiting. With his bulk, he would have great difficulty in turning round in his chair to face his visitor.

There was no sound from in there. And the girl was surprised at how softly the big man moved. He made no more noise than she did in her soft shoes and that was very little noise at all.

Twilight was a mite deaf. Would he hear anything? Halo made a motion for her to stay behind him and she did so. She didn't know what else to do.

Halo moved into the main room in which Twilight sat.

The armchair was there, the broken stairs looping off to the left of it. Twilight was on the armchair, but he wasn't actually sitting in it. He had turned around and had one knee on the seat and was facing Halo as the big man approached.

Halo's gun wasn't level. He halted. Too late he saw the chunky double-barrelled pistol in Twilight's fat fist.

Halo raised his Colt. But that as Twilight actually fired. A double-triggered derringer-type pistol—and both triggers pulled at once.

The little gun—and it was small even though bigger and heavier than the average standard derringer—had a kick like a horse and was a lot better at close quarters. But this was close enough—and Halo took both slugs in the full of his broad, muscular chest.

His Colt went up in the air and he banged back into the girl, almost knocking her off her feet. She was on her knees when Halo's big bulk hit the floor beside her.

She scrambled to her feet. 'He made me ...'

'I know,' said Twilight, gently.

Outside, voices were shouting. But nobody was coming into the house.

The posse was in good sight of the ghost town like a cluster of large broken boxes thrown down in the waste and the brilliant sunshine.

Dack Simms, who used to be Sam Dacson, thought he recognized this ruinous place as the place where he had killed an arrogant kid gunfighter called Dale Consarn. But—he told himself—he couldn't really be sure.

Maybe he was peering harder than his companions, trying to make up his mind, though he wasn't sure why he should feel he had to do that. Make his mind up, that is ...

He said, 'I thought I saw somep'n move on the edge there.'

Abe Codine said, 'Spread out. Keep your heads down. Let's go.' He veered his horse over to the right, away from back. The other riders were splitting up already, spreading out. This was a disciplined bunch.

They went into the town at different angles, almost catching the bandits on the hop, though they had been given warning by the man Dack Simms had spotted on the edge of the tumble-down edifices. He had been minding the horses. The beasts had been left where they were. The look-out-cum-minder was, like his *compadres*, hunting cover, finding hidden shooting space.

Twenty-Three

Twilight said, 'You never call me "Uncle" when we're on our own. Only when we're in the stores an' there are other folk ...'

'The store's gone,' said the girl. 'It's behind us.' But she still sounded bewildered and shocked.

There was shouting outside. The two shots that had killed Halo must have been heard. But nobody had come to investigate.

'They've been startled,' Twilight said. 'I figure some other folk have turned up. A posse I guess. What else could it be? Somebody must've told 'em where we'd be. Maybe this was not a good idea, you an' me coming here. But I've had stuff stashed here, y'know.' It wasn't like the devious, arrogant fat man to admit a mistake he might have made.

'It's all in there now,' he went on, pointing downwards. He was standing up now. 'That we brought with us as well. We've got to get out of here.'

The carpet-bag was under the armchair in which Twilight had been sitting.

'We can't get out,' said Lucy. 'I hear somebody out back as well.'

Twilight took up the bulging carpet-bag, looking about him as if seeking a loophole. 'We should've had the carriage nearer.'

'We hid it, didn't we?' Lucy looked towards the front of the shattered building. The sounds from out there seemed to be nearer, louder. Shots sounded, but they seemed a mite further away. Twilight moved, lightly for so heavy a man, swinging the carpet-bag, making for the rickety staircase.

'We'll get up here.'

He began to climb. Lucy looked alarmed. But she began to follow him. They could be trapped. But, then again, there could be some means of getting out and down from up there.

She was only on the third step when the staircase groaned like an animal in pain, as an animal that had had too much weight put upon it.

Lucy was propelled backwards. She hit the floor, sprawled. Loose timbers narrowly missed her as the bottom half of the staircase came down, piecemeal.

Looking up, Lucy saw that Twilight had made the top, saw his twinkling small feet in their modish shoes. It was as if he had dressed for an occasion, this was it; but it had gone more than slightly awry.

But the fat man had had a bit of luck so far, Lady Luck making amends. From the back Lucy had called him 'Uncle': thus he'd deduced there was somebody with her, and he had been able to put Halo down.

Had Twilight expected Halo and the rest to get here so soon? Had he expected Halo at all? It hadn't seemed like it: all that boodle—and flying free.

From his position on the floor Halo grinned at her with dead, staring eyes.

She rose. A man came into the room. One of Halo's comrades, seeing the girl, seeing the body. Twilight was out of sight, quiet like a flying mouse in an eyrie.

The man cursed and grabbed the girl. She raised her hands, fingers bent like talons, nails slashing.

Lucky Twilight. He wasn't even watching now.

The talons clawed at the man's face, narrowly missing his eyes. He shouted in pain and staggered backwards. Then the girl was away from him.

She was wild, reckless. She ran for the back. Across the ruined kitchen, through the open apology for a door.

There were two men and she ran right into them.

Deputy Bill Legwell. And the second man she recognized as the enigmatic Dack Simms. She didn't know him well. He was the same man ... but, somehow, he didn't look the same man any more.

'Hold her,' he said, and the young deputy held her. She sagged in his arms, all fight leaving her.

Dack went through the doorway, through the kitchen.

Another door, just a gap really. And a man coming at him. A bleeding face. A gun in hand. But Dack had also had his gun in his hand all the time, though its pearl-handled twin was still ensconced in its holster.

He elevated the muzzle. He pressed the trigger.

One quick shot. But it found a mark. At such short distance the slug ploughed a path right through the other man's shoulder, came out the other side, spent, but driving the man with it. It left him. He hit the floor, his eyes glazing over as he passed out.

Outside, the gunfire seemed to reach a crescendo and then virtually died.

Nobody else in this indoor room except Dack Simms and his unconscious adversary who wouldn't be any trouble any more.

Then Dack sensed a movement. Above him.

He lifted his head, was surprised to see the grotesque, hanging half-staircase.

But a face above it in a shattered gap. And the barrel of a gun.

Two barrels.

Twilight had loaded his pistol. He fired one barrel.

Dack was flinging himself to one side. He heard the slug go past his head like a diving, angry bumblebee. He could almost hear the breath of it. He rolled, came up into a sitting position, surprised even that he'd actually hit the floor.

A dead man lying near grinned at him. Then he was triggering his Colt, the barrel like a pointing finger.

The bullets streamed up at the gap, and wooden slivers and plaster and dust showered down.

In the gap the fat face of Twilight appeared, eyes staring, mouth agape, gun in one hand, what looked like a carpetbag in the other.

He dropped both the bag and the gun. The bag thudded heavily as it hit the boards below. It was almost as if Twilight had meant to return it to whoever its contents had belonged.

The chunky little gun hit the boards with a clatter.

Twilight said something in a high-pitched voice. If he was making words, they made no sense to the man below who still pointed his gun upwards, though he didn't need it now.

Twilight went backwards. His face disappeared. Only one dead hand hung limply over the edge of the jagged gap as the grotesque staircase angled up there, seemed to be vibrating.

But it was still. Everything was suddenly still, almost quiet. No more gunfire. Subdued voices outside.

Dack Simms holstered his single gun, matching it to its twin on the other hip. He picked up the carpet-bag and opened it.

It was stuffed with money and jewellery.

He let it fall with a thump. He looked up at the half-staircase. The rest of it lay as debris around his feet.

He looked up at the jagged gap and the limp, dead, well-manicured hand; and his plain face was expressionless.

Slowly he unbuckled the gunbelt with both of the elegant pearl-handled guns and he rolled the complete rig into a sort of bundle.

He swung the bundle high, calculatingly, and he let it go. It sailed through the gap, passing the limp white hand without touching it. There was a thump and the lethal bundle was out of sight and the dust settled.

Dack Simms turned away.

The posse was going home. Its casualties were small, unimportant. It had prisoners. They rode their own horses. They had their wrists tied in front of them so they could still guide the beasts. They were made to ride in front of the troop, the girl Lucy among them in like fashion.

The posse-members rode unspeaking until Sheriff Abel Codine turned to his friend, Dack Simms, and asked softly, 'What happened to your guns, *amigo?*'

Just as softly, Dack said, 'The fat man's looking after 'em for me.'

The woman and the man sat on their horses in the green peace of the knoll, so close to the waste of the badlands if they looked downwards and in a certain direction.

But they were not looking in that direction, rather at the plains the other side, a sea of green, broken by brown sections and the lighter patches of rock and, here and there, a few trees.

This was cattle country, prime Texas grazing land with small creeks, most of them washing down to the Rio Conchos or the Big Red.

They were Westerners through and through, both of them, and this was where, in a land like this, they would always want to be.

They had come up here a lot in the last few weeks, meeting at the man's place and then going on from there, letting their horses meander, taking their time.

They had talked. Always they had talked. They had delighted themselves and each other with the old lingo, the Western phrases and the border *patois*.

They both knew, however, that things would never again be as they were. Their own relationship was closer, but too many other things obtruded now. Terrible things that had been done and could never be undone.

She was still a young girl, younger than the man not only in age but also in experience, immeasurably so.

She knew in her heart that soon he

would go, had always known this.

She knew that he had already been invited by an elderly friend to take over management of a horse ranch outside Sante Fe. She knew that he was planning to let another friend—in Sandela—take over his little spread, although the girl's father would gladly have done so and paid a higher price.

Her father had changed, as the girl and the man had changed. None of them would ever be quite the same again, though maybe in some ways they would be strangely better. The girl was more mature, the older and younger man more tolerant and settled in their minds, the one to stay, the other to go.

And this, at last, was the day.

They were silent now as they looked out at the land; he as if he were drinking it in.

'It would never be the same,' he had said earlier. 'Not here.'

'It doesn't have to be here,' she had said,

and he had accepted the feeling in her that had made her say this, loving her father as she did.

He had told her that morning that he had accepted the job at Sante Fe. He had brought her here and would leave her here so that she could watch him go.

At last, she did this, watching him, erect in the saddle, riding out over that green sea.

He turned and waved to her once and she waved back. Then he and the horse were a moving blob on the green immensity, and then the small sight of them was hidden by the veil of tears in her eyes.

But then she smiled and she raised her hand in a salute which he would not see and she whispered, 'Soon I will see you. But soon, *querida.*' And she gave a click with her tongue and the horse moved.

This Large Print Book for the Partially sighted, who cannot read normal print, is published under the auspices of

THE ULVERSCROFT FOUNDATION